No Forwarding Address

by
Della Van Hise

Eye Scry Publications

ISBN: 978-1-942415-01-5
Eye Scry Publications

Many other Eye Scry Publications are available at a substantial volume discount to bookstores, libraries, etc. Please visit our website at www.eyescrypublications.com

For Wendy...

who brought me back from the dead.

When Terrans came to sail dark seas
And see what stars might be,
Heaven moved with no forwarding address...
And left this void to me.
—Children's song from Lazali

9th May, 2184
Beloved Crystal,

Forgive me. I write this in the 4th Class Passenger's section on the Lunar Transport, *Dorsai*, and though the flight is only five hours old, I have already begun to wonder if my decision to leave Terra was a rational one. I know only that the act of leaving you was a painful one; all else is secondary.

But now that I do not have to look into your face, now that I do not have to feel the anguish we have shared, perhaps I can explain why I have chosen this course of action. Not that explanations will ease the pain or erase the guilt, but possibly these words might allow both of us to sleep a trifle easier.

Fogg is with me – ah, poor Fogg. He tells me that he will be starting a novel soon – a novel about us, about the absurdity of life on Terra, and the cruel irony of life in general. He misses you, Crystal, almost as much as I, and says he will immortalize in words what we could never have in reality. If you would like, I shall send chapters of his novel as he writes them. It is his wish – and mine, of course – that you share this voyage with us even though you cannot be here physically. I know now that I should have told you of my plans to board the *Dorsai*; I understand that perhaps I should have remained on Terra's shattered soil with you and abandoned this fanatical dream of mine. But I do not know if you would have been able to respect me (or I myself) if I had done so. And, ultimately, I feared that my restlessness would have torn us apart just as efficiently as the War snuffed out the redwings and butterflies and small spring flowers which grew on grassy hills but had no name. Utopia, after all, is fragile and transient, and despite what we might have once believed, ours was no different.

The *Dorsi*, is crowded here in our section, and one need only look around to know that my dream is not the unique one I once perceived it to be. The faces in 4th Class are filled with uneasiness and pain and memories a thousand centuries old. All these people are running, Crystal – either toward or away from someone or something – and I am no longer certain there is a difference. Running is the same anywhere and always, and I suspect that I am the greatest runner of all.

The woman in the G-bunk across the aisle from me cries silently, tears slipping from her haunted eyes then floating up into the weightlessness of the cabin. No one seems to notice, other than Fogg, of course, who has been curled soundlessly against my side since our journey began. He feels too much, you know, and for that I cannot help but be sorry for him.

Empathy must certainly be the worst "gift" of all – to be eternally open to the pain and hurt and lonely tears of all those with whom he comes in contact. His stray thoughts inform me that the crying woman is bound for Luna to die; that she, like so many of us, has grown heartsick over Terra, and is making the final voyage to Luna – where euthanasia is permitted and almost as common as black market Amnesia Merchants. Fogg says she will find her peace, her release from memories of loved ones; and perhaps her decision is the sanest any of us could make. But as you well know, Fogg is somewhat of a sad romantic. He is no more ready to lie down in some sterile room and inhale pleasantly scented poison than you or I. His empathic abilities are simply too powerful for his own good; and he cannot help but feel and think what the crying woman is feeling and thinking.

But as to the purpose of this journey... you must know that I had no choice in this matter. For longer than I can recall, I have ached for something – just as you have confessed to aching to return to your South Florida home of childhood. For me, the pain, the longing, and the compulsion were for space – for the stars, for a "home" to which I have never been. Perhaps I am simply mad; and quite probably I have sacrificed the most important thing I ever found: you. And yet, I maintain that I had no alternative within *myself*. As long as the ache remained alive within me, I could not have loved you as you deserved and needed to be loved. The ache, and whatever secret might lie behind it, would always exist as a wall between us.

I know, Crystal, that I am not truly Terran; and if that belief constitutes a madman, then I openly confess to insanity. Who I really am, I do not yet know, and that is why I had to leave Earth and you. To find out. I seem to have memories which go beyond the span of my own life – memories of a place and a people to whom I belong. The images are blurred with time and distance (and perhaps an alternate dimension or two), but they are nonetheless real.

I see faces as I sleep, and I must know to whom those faces belong. There are, of course, whimsical legends of extraterrestrials having been on Terra for centuries, but it is not precisely in this direction which my own thoughts travel. You see, my beloved, I cannot recall the childhood I must have had... somewhere or somewhen. I cannot recall walking by the sea or carrying a broken cane pole to a secret pond to fish. I have no recollection of childhood friends nor parents nor Sunday Schools, nor anything at all before I reached the biological age of thirty. So you see, my dearest friend, I have been thirty all my life, and will continue to be thirty until I die.

And there is an ironic frustration in immortality.

I feel secure in sharing these feelings with you, for you are one of the few who never passed judgment upon my mental wanderings. But I am telling you things we have discussed a hundred times before, and there is no real need to repeat myself, other than perhaps to help you understand why I have taken this first step of a trek which will – hopefully – bring the answers.

And that is really the purpose of life, is it not? (Or at least that is what we Terrans have told ourselves – that answers are the only thing we'll ever really be able to possess). I do not know what questions to ask, nor precisely where I am going once we reach Lunaport. But if I am fortunate, I hope I will find your answers in addition to my own. I am hopeful that alien science will discover some means whereby to immunize you to the peculiar germs of space so that you may join me one day soon on Altair or Regulus or Cephalon IX.

And that, too, is the purpose of Fogg's proposed novel – to explore those ironies of our lives. I cannot help but experience a certain amount of bitterness connected to the fact that you (you, my beloved lover of the stars) are among those few Terrans who cannot leave Earth. Medical science has mastered almost every technique, save one that would give you the protection you would need to survive naturally. Fogg maintains that serums will soon be developed which would strengthen your immunities, and I am forced to believe him. Please believe with me, love, for I am also enough of a romantic to think that the mind is capable of magic which science shall never have the ability to duplicate.

Did anyone ever tell you that multiple G-forces appear to facilitate hallucinations? I'd heard the theory and the rumors, but had never placed much faith in them until we lifted off from Port Nevada. Perhaps it was a combination of not eating and spending too many hours waiting in the 125° desert heat, but I must admit that I experienced something most peculiar during our liftoff. As I've mentioned, our section is painfully crowded; and once you're strapped into a G-bunk breathing a mixture of oxygen and nitrogen, things can get a little distorted of their own accord. There are two children directly behind us, and Fogg was nervous about being in close proximity to their potentially uncontrollable fear during the liftoff. He jokingly (if Fogg can be said to joke) says that children are the bravest and the most cowardly of all sentient animals; and I suspect his empathy was simply working overtime in the cramped conditions.

There are approximately ninety passengers crammed into this section which was originally designed to carry no more than sixty. A baby was crying, and two old men with wrinkled faces and frightened eyes were arguing about which of them was to get the window seat. I found myself lost in the atmosphere and the thoughts of the people around me, and once the *Dorsai* finally got around to hoisting up her skinny metal legs and thrusting herself bravely out into the black uterus of space, I'd started to drift in alpha. Fogg insists that some of these older ships still pipe nitrous oxide into the oxygen mixture just to keep the passengers from realizing that they're about to hurl their fragile biological forms out into unforgiving darkness, and for once I believe Fogg is right.

When the G-forces climbed to about 4 is when everything came together – or fell apart – depending, I suppose, on one's point of view. I suddenly found myself back on Terra, before the War that turned green to gray and fantasies to nightmares, and murdered children with as little conscience as it obliterated slug worms and poisonous vipers. But at least one thing can be said for the bombs: they possessed no sense of prejudice. I am glad, my beloved, that you did not live in the time of the War. I am glad you never heard the sound of a whale, for now you do not have to mourn its absence from the Earth.

But as I was saying... as the *Dorsai* sluggishly lifted into stagnant Nevada air, I was somehow transported back in time. My mind took me to a place I have never been before – a place in a desert on a world that was not Terra. You were by my side, and for a time we walked through the sand and did nothing more than watch a blue sunset and listen to the sounds of some immense city in the distance. And the horrifying thing, Crystal, was that the sounds of that city were no different from the sounds of any city anywhere.

There was a cry of sirens in the streets, and the bark of frightened dogs. There was silence and madness and moments when the two combined. It was an asylum somewhere out there among the countless stars, and the answer to all questions was insanity. Madness was the only safe haven, the only refuge, the only and ultimate answer.

Needless to say, I am somewhat more optimistic about the real voyage than this hallucinated one. But the pleasant thing was that you were with me; and even when reality returned I could not help remembering how it used to be.

Ah, Crystal, there were so many years that passed before I met you, so many times I would watch you in secret when you were still essentially a child. So many times I wanted to love you and do nothing else. And for awhile, I was safe in that fantasized version of reality.

Perhaps this is the most painful thing I will ever say to anyone: the dream could not withstand. A man may love a woman for a time, but eventually the deeper mysteries of life will come to claim him. Eventually, beloved, the pull of space becomes too powerful, and Man is compelled to leave behind the warmth, the memory of an embrace and the gentle scent of Terran summers. And that, again, is the ultimate irony. If I had been in my right mind, I never could have left you; so perhaps you are better off without my uncertainties and insecurities and fanatical searches for answers that might not exist in any universe or dimension.

If only you could be here now – now that the hallucination is ended and the grim gray reality of the transport has materialized solidly around me.

The crying woman has spent all her tears it. Only her dull blue eyes show evidence that she is haunted by the universal mockery living in all of us. Were it not for Fogg's stray thoughts, I might now perceive her to be some middle-aged secretary in transit to a position with Calchem on Lunaport.

The two children who so terrified Fogg at the onset of our journey are quietly eating stale sandwiches brought from Terra, and whispering about young ladies of questionable character whom they would like to sexually impale. The old men who were haggling over the coveted window seat have both drifted into uneasy slumber, and their snores sound remarkably like some purring tomcat sleeping near the hearth. Only the infant still cries, and perhaps there is some significance to that. For he, too, has left his home, not knowing where destiny will eventually abandon him.

I must close now, love, and attempt to comfort our friend, Fogg. Though he slept for awhile, he has awakened and informs me that my morose state of mind is disturbing his "space". Ah, poor Fogg, He never should have attempted this journey with me, yet he, too, claims to feel the pull of Mother Space.

We will find our answers, beloved one, and perhaps we will be home to Terra again before the spring flowers come to life in your treasured South Florida next year. If there was one miracle Terra ever experienced, it was the fact that the bombs left some things untouched – and that there are still a few secret places where flowers can grow and birds can eat natural grains without laying soft-shelled eggs, and two lonely cats can howl on fence posts in humid spring evenings when the moon is nearly full. Perhaps that is the only miracle there ever was or will be. That, and whatever magic you and I shared for the time allotted to us on Terra.

Until....
Raine
Communication #DEC.978419.Dorsai

PS – Let me know if you want to see Fogg's novel once he begins composing it. And, for that matter, let me know if I'll ever hear from you again. I honestly would not blame you if you chose to seek out an Amnesia Merchant and forget you ever knew me. Perhaps that would be a fitting punishment indeed. I am sorry, love... for both of us.

———

12th May, 2184
Raine,

You probably won't believe me when I tell you this, but I knew I couldn't keep you from the moment we first met. And, if possible, I think I knew why. So if it's any consolation to either of us, perhaps that inner knowledge has made your departure a little easier to accept.

I <u>had</u> considered doing as I thought you might – going to the local market and finding someone with little enough scruples to administer an Amnesia Merchant. But what would I have then? Not even the memories, Raine. And memories, like questions, are the only things either of us seem to possess right now. If I seem bitter and self-pitying, it is because I am. After all, It's the "Me" generation again, and the shrinks seem to think a little maudlin self-suffering is good for the soul (though they remain unable or unwilling to define what the 'soul' might even pretend to <u>be</u>).

By the time you receive this, you will be far away from Lunaport, and for that I am grateful. Collette (you remember her, don't you?) had to spend two weeks at Lunaport last summer; and while she did manage to escape with her life intact, it took several months for her to completely recover her wits and reassess her personal morals.

But what troubles me most is not knowing where you are. At least whenever we were apart on Terra, I was safe in the knowledge that the same sun sent the same warmth and light to you as it did to me. I was content to know that by the air we breathed, we were somehow connected at all times. Terra formed the bond, but now even that union is severed and I wonder if we will ever be able to recapture it. Granted, the same stars shine on Earth as shine on Altair or Regulus, but some say that starlight, though beautiful, is cold and lonely, and that those who crave it are doomed to become part of that same icy emptiness. I hope you are different, Raine. I hope you are stronger than legends.

You needn't apologize for your "insanity." It's a common disease here on Terra, and I'm convinced that we are <u>all</u> quite mad in one manner or another. Your particular brand name of lunacy is no *more or less frightening than anyone else's. You said you had no alternative but to leave Terra, and I am compelled to believe you. If nothing else, I know that you have never lied to me, and never intentionally to yourself. You believe your own mind, and for that strength and confidence, I have envied you. And yet, I wonder if the answers you seek are possible to find, or if they are entirely subjective interpretations of questionable facts.*

You must realize that at least 90% of all Terrans have wondered about their ancestry since the first man first crawled out of the sea (or disembarked from his shiny spacecraft). I know and accept that you are different, love. You once told me that you had lived on Terra since before the War, which would make you at least 150 years old. I do not dispute your claims, nor do I require proof of them, in spite of the fact that the oldest man on Earth right now is only a little over 50. The doctors are proud of the old son-of-a-bitch. I heard a news report yesterday suggesting that his ability to combat the low-level radiation might offer some kind of hope for the rest of us.

Ah well, I suppose wars have a tendency to leave their consequences lying around, and it shouldn't be any surprise that the life-expectancy has decreased. It's good that you're gone, Raine. I wouldn't want to see you thrown into a sterile room to become a living experiment. But what I'm saying is that perhaps there's some other explanation for your longevity – some explanation aside from extraterrestrial origins. Since you paint yourself as the romantic who believes in the ultimate power of the mind, perhaps there really isn't any great mystery about your lifespan. You simply refused to accept a death sentence imposed by lunatics who drop bombs for a living. You wanted more time, and you gave it to yourself. Period.

Then again, it's entirely possible that I'm wrong. Fogg isn't particularly romantic in the same sense of the word, yet he's been by yourself for nearly as long as you can remember. You're two old men who forgot how to die... maybe because Terra never really let you live. I just hope I'm as healthy as either one of you when I'm a hundred and fifty! Sometimes I have to laugh at images I see in my mind – you and Fogg wandering off through the forest, staring in wonder at some gypsy moth while the great mother ship lifted off without you.

In many selfish ways, I'm sorry we live in the times we do. If we'd lived over two hundred years ago, you would not have left Terra, for the technology which has taken you to Lunaport and beyond would not have existed. Your dreams and your restlessness would have been there, but the means whereby to separate us (forever?) would have been too far in the future even to conceive. Perhaps dreams were safer then, for they would have been consigned forever to the impossible. You might have run away for a time to join the Peace Corps (or maybe the Hare Krishnas?) but we would still have remained joined by Terra herself. Selfishly, that is my wish.

Yours is an old soul, I fear, a soul that will never be content to stay in one place too long. I see you as a man who has lived many lives – and I do not speak in the metaphysical sense of reincarnation. You are the ultimate vagabond, Raine – a man who is not capable of permitting roots to grow too deep for fear that the pain will be equally as deep when they are finally exhumed. Do not forget, love, that though I am far younger than you, my psychic talents are occasionally as strong. (Or so I like to tell myself when we are apart. It makes being "with" you so much easier.)

You see, the reason I always understood you so well was because I am very much like you. No, I have not lived three normal lifetimes as you have, but my "home" is not somewhere on this lonely ball of blue and green seasons hanging at the edge of a galaxy gone mad. It comes to memory that Man first developed the ability to travel beyond the solar system just over a hundred years ago. Just after the War ended, the first intelligent species was discovered on one of the Altairian planets. I grew up with that knowledge, Raine, with the knowledge that there is other life in the universe. I grew up knowing that it might one day be possible to dine on Altairian lobster in the evening and Regulan fire-fish the following morning, and stop off at Lunaport before returning home to Terra to sleep. The stars and the otherworlds were never a dream to me. They were always a reality. I knew when I was nine that I had to go there when I was older. I used to look at the stars and try to imagine what worlds were circling those points of light, and what kind of life form might be looking back at me through some cheap telescope. I daydreamed of going "out there" and picking wildflowers on Centauri when I was older...

Ah, Raine, do children everywhere live for that moment when they become adults, then spend the rest of their lives attempting to recapture what they had when they were children? That is something you must tell me about when you've had the opportunity to travel about the galaxy for awhile. I want to know if the children on Nineva IV skip through dew-covered grass on cool mornings just as the children do here on Terra. I want to know if the children of Axial capture injured birds with broken wings and nurse them back to health, only to have the frightened creature die quietly in an alien night. And I want to know if the children on Cephalon IX lie awake on hot summer evenings, dreaming about adventures and forts made of palm fronds and invisible friends whom parents cannot perceive. Tell me all these things, Raine, for I do want to share your journey.

And if you should ever discover a world where science has perfected a way to immunize us fragile humans from the treacherous diseases which Wars everywhere have created, let me know of that, too, and I <u>will</u> meet you on Altair or Regulus before senility takes away the memories of our time together. Gods, I fear that most of all! Growing old, alone, and losing more of you every moment.

And in that way, I think I can comprehend how your life has been, and perhaps even how it is destined to be. Fogg once told me that you have known many lovers – that you have shared the warmth and the bed of a hundred women and a few men over the years, and that your greatest pain was watching them grow old while you remained young and beautiful and unmarred by the years. But do not forget <u>their</u> pain. Do not forget the anguish your old lovers must have experienced once they realized <u>your</u> truth, my love. For now I understand both sides. Now that I am another of your loves, now that our minds and bodies have met and merged, I think I knew what it was like for them, and for you. And the cruelest part is that Time did not treat you as equals. Perhaps growing old together would not be so frightening a thing, but watching the years strip away the memory and the beauty of only one... That is the most vicious cruelty my mind can conceive.

And the saddest thing perhaps is that anyone who has known you as intimately as I have will never again be free. Your mind is a powerful and addictive drug, Raine, and though I understand that now, I do not know if I possess the strength to prevent Time from taking you away from me – for Time as a protective and jealous mistress who will guard her consort well.

After I discovered that you had left our apartment in San Diego, I began making plans to return to Florida. After all, without you it was too painful to stay in the company of so many memories. The rocky beaches and carved stone faces and deserted freeways with stubborn blades of grass growing in the grooves were all too close, too much of a reminder that your feet no longer walk upon this earth. Pizza at Scarzella's became an impossibility, for I discovered that I could not walk through the doors without expecting to see you in that dark corner booth where so many memories took shape for us.

And so, love, as of next week I'm going home – back to the barn where we first met and the house where I grew up and which seems to protect me a little more from our memories. Nothing in comparison to your journey, I realize, but of equal importance until such time as science sees fit to provide an answer to my immunity problem. You see, it isn't that I never shared your dreams. It's just that I wasn't allowed, through genetics or Fate, to give them a chance. And knowing that I <u>couldn't</u> was the worse trick of all. As with you, the stars and space feel implanted in my every thought... but so are the chromosomes or dormant genes (or galactic demon) which keep me from them. Rather like giving a starving child a thick steak for dinner, only to inform him just prior to his first bite that it's merely a cardboard replica. Fogg should have a marvelous time attempting to explain <u>that</u> irony!

But rest assured that my best wishes and my love are always with you. I hope you can find your home and that it will not turn out to be a cardboard steak. And if you do find it, you must tell me what it is like, this world which neither of us have ever seen. You must tell me of the sunsets and moonrises and dream merchants and dark deserted streets with stray dogs howling in the night.

Most of all, take care and try not to think lonely thoughts. I shall live with the hope that you'll return to Terra; but if you never do, then please find something close to happiness out there in all that darkness.

Still and always,
Crystal
Communication #4187442.Orlando.DAYE

PS – Yes, do transmit Fogg's novel. While I don't normally like to be kept in suspense waiting for the next chapters of a serial, I do want to know what dear Fogg thought of our escapades. I presume he'll also be writing of your adventures among the ruins of space, so tell him to get on with it! Life is so short!

20th May, 2184
Altair VII

Beloved Crystal,

I thought I had learned to be patient. However, I am beginning to discover that my patience is quite thin. After I reached Lunaport and prepared to depart for Altair, I started to wonder if I would ever receive word from you again. I have questioned my own mental stability recently, and am still unconvinced (despite Fogg's gentle claims to the contrary) that I am a rational being. Perhaps in some way, despite the initial pain, catching the *Dorsai* to Lunaport was relatively easy. From there, from Luna City with its spires and industrial smokestacks which give off no vapors in the absence of atmosphere, it would have been a mere nineteen hour flight back to Terra and you. But once we boarded the *Sandstorm* bound for Altair, I knew that I was completely mad.

Fogg informs me that I was kept sedated for much of the journey. When I awakened the last time, after quite a bout with nightmares and the traditional virgin spacer's dreams of darkness, it was to find myself here, on Altair, in a somewhat less than reputable hotel on the South Side. Fogg was bending over me, attempting to rouse me back to unmerciful consciousness. In many ways, love, I wish he had not succeeded, for in that blackness of slumber, dreams crossed the void back to you with ease. And yet, when it came to mind to tell Fogg that I wished to return to Earth, I discovered that this ache is still present within me. I have seen the stars, Crystal, but the hunger is still in me – the need, the pain, the persistent compulsion to find whatever it is that makes a home.

We have been on Altair for one full day (37 hours by their method of timekeeping) , and so far I have no reason to believe I am any closer to finding that home than I was back on Terra a hundred years ago. And in that knowledge, in that despair, I cannot help but believe I have made a grave error. And yet, how does one go back? Surely if I returned to Earth now, I would always have the doubt in my mind, the gnawing which whispered that I did not go *far* enough, that I did not search *long* enough, that I did not try to the best of whatever ability I possess. Circles. Life is a conglomeration of circles and doubts and mistakes and whispers from some dark corner of one's immortal soul.

When the whispers are silenced, then I will know that I have found whatever I am seeking. Until then....

The hotel where we are staying is oddly barbaric. But the beds are clean and the management doesn't object to Fogg's telepathic and empathic abilities. I have heard that some worlds expressly forbid telepaths, and we are in the process of attempting to discover which worlds have such laws – some research I *should* have done before I left Earth, but my impetuous nature has once again thwarted any practicality I might once have possessed.

There are six other tenants in our wing at the moment, and Fogg has discovered that several others will be moving in tomorrow morning. Our own room is like some tenements in New York or Chicago or any other large city on Terra before the War. There is a bed which creaks in angry protest as we sleep; there are four walls, no hot water, and the paint has long since faded from pale green to naked transparency.

The woman across the hall is a rather questionable medium of sorts. It is amusing to watch her clients coming and going at all hours, and to listen to the moans, bumps, rapping and tapping from her even more questionable séances. There are no laws here forbidding exploitation of the weak-minded, and shingles are hung on every corner of every busy street. The signs advertise everything from palm readers to mind readers to card readers to those who will read cracks in the sidewalk or cloud patterns in the sky. So the woman is breaking no laws; she is simply doing what she must in order to survive – taking money from the disheartened souls who have lost someone very dear to them.

Her name is Maddiae, and she is perhaps fifty Terran years of age. She wears a faded headband across her brow, claiming that it was given to her by a river witch on Resaurius, and that the spirits speak to her through the golden threads woven through the band's black leather. Ah, love, I saw the same headband in the lobby of our hotel; if one turns it wrong side out, it becomes a souvenir of Altair.

Fogg says that Maddiae has never been offworld, never met a river witch, but that she means no one harm. I feel sorry for her, Crystal. Perhaps because she represents what I might have become if things had turned out differently. She is alone and frightened and embittered over the fact that she was not looked upon kindly by the cosmos, and so she spends her time fabricating answers and messages for others. She says she will do a reading for me free of charge, but I am afraid of what she might see. Fogg says I should not go.

The children are playing in the narrow streets now, and it is close to dusk with the scent of someone's dinner drifting through my open window. Were it not for the launchport on the horizon and the constant rear of the rockets, it would be easy to believe that this was Terra herself – before the War, before the Technology Race... *before*. The sun is setting red in a purple sky, and my thoughts keep returning to an afternoon on the beach in Coronado – when you and I were insignificant black silhouettes, when there was nothing more important than holding you close and making love with the sea's whisper for our orchestra.

But more than that, I find myself returning to your childhood – to memories of watching you become the woman you are, to the ache of knowing that you were soon to meet and be possessed by a man who did not deserve you. Ah, beloved, the sunset here reminds me of that so very much that the bittersweet pain is easily remembered now. I had observed you secretly for so long that perhaps I believed no one else had a right to be near you in any manner whatsoever. And yet, the evening came when you fell in love that first time... with a man you hardly knew, and later married and later divorced and later learned to despise.

Do you remember it? Perhaps neither of us wants to now, and perhaps I am foolish to mention it at all. I watched you leave your Florida house on the night of your wedding, watched you walk the ceremonial path to the white arches by the lake, watched you give yourself into marriage. And I wished, love, oh how I ached to be the man who would take you home. But you did not even know that I existed then. To you I was nothing more than a shadow behind a willow tree – something you thought you had seen out the corner of your eye, but which seemed to disappear when you turned for a second glance. You ware fifteen then... fifteen when you married... and I was already a very old man.

Forgive me for my digression, but some things must be said, and old feelings are the only ones I seem to have right now. Also, I fear I am somewhat nervous about addressing your letter directly. Not because of what you have said, but because of what I am afraid to say in response.

If it is possible, I believe I knew you were like myself from the beginning.

And perhaps that is what drew us together so strongly – the sense of displacement, the longing for somewhere to belong. And yet, by loving you, I have condemned you to the

20

pain of loss, of separation. I had known for some time that my lifespan is greater than yours, yet I selfishly loved you anyway. At first, from a distance and in anonymity, there was no harm to anyone other than myself. But when I came to you in the open, I condemned you. For when you began to return my feelings in your innocence, perhaps we both believed that what we had would last forever. Perhaps it will, love. *Somehow*... it must.

Again, forgive me. My mind is wandering and the hour is late, and the children are still playing in the dark and dirty streets beneath my window. Thinking is difficult for me at this moment, and I perceive this is due to the difference in the energy field between Terra and Altair. In truth, I am displaced. Yet I feel this has always been true – even in the corn fields of Earth and at Lunaport and in all the darkness which lies between realities.

There are two boys and a girl, all between the ages of seven and nine Terran years. They are tossing a clear plastic ball back and forth to one another, and I am jealous of their joy. That is what I am searching for, beloved: the memories I have lost, the childhood that does not exist in my memory, the puppies and kittens and small friends I cannot recall. You can understand that, can't you? I am searching for the child I was who is no direct relation to the man I am; and possibly once they are joined I can rest. I can only hope that it will not be too late – for you and for me and for Terra.

We depart Altair in one week. By that time, Fogg and I should have earned enough credits to cover passage to Regulus. There is a rumor that medical science there is further advanced than on Earth, so perhaps we can be together again soon. Or perhaps whatever home I am seeking *is* Regulus. I do not believe so, as I have viewed holos of the systems there; and aside from the vast loneliness of the Regulan Dune Sea, there is no sense of familiarity.

And if Regulus is not the answer, we will have to book passage on toward the outer worlds and try to find a Sleeper ship with room for two passengers who possess little money and less common sense.

Fogg says he is looking forward to four months of utter silence in the mind; and I must admit a certain fondness for that idea myself. At the very least, I am told that the drugs administered on the Sleepers produce vivid dreams, and that for an additional fee one may purchase a device which allows one to dream lucidly. In that manner, love, I will be with you again very soon.

Until...
Raine
Communication: 8833829.Validate.DEX

PS – Fogg is just now completing notes on the first chapter of his novel. I have read passages of his work, and almost wish I had not. Sometimes the beauty of love, when in the past, is too painful to bear.

30th May, 2184
Central Florida

Raine,
Damn you! Damn you for your dreams and your searches and your questions and your compulsion to find all the answers in a single lifetime no matter what the cost! Whatever we had, whatever made us unique is only half real without you, and though it is self-serving sorrow I cannot help the way I am feeling in this angry moment in the middle of a hot pre-summer night which is suddenly very cold.
When I first learned of your departure for Lunaport, perhaps I was arrogant enough to believe your journey would begin and end there – that you would come to understand that answers alone will never be enough. What are we, after all, but creatures who spend our

too-short lives in search of <u>love</u>? But you, dear Raine, have abandoned what we found – that ultimate Terran treasure – to search for something intangible and possibly even unreal! I do not know if that makes you a fool or an extremely brave and wise man, and I'm not at all certain that I want to know. Some answers are less destructive when left as questions.

I look into the sky at night, and it isn't difficult to see those fragile ships crawling around the firmament like infants in some universal crib. And though it is impossible for the human eye to cross such expanses, I occasionally wonder if one of those pale white lights contains you, and if you are looking back toward Earth. But more often, I wonder if you even <u>want</u> to look back toward Terra at all. She was always such an embarrassment to you, wasn't she? And perhaps now that you have washed your hands of her, you are finally free. Or is it possible that you have become a mere slave to the inherent madness of Man?

Ah, Raine, despite your years and your wisdom, there is so much you do not understand. Whether you came from the womb of some Terran whore or the wife of a president or were merely the product of a romantic accident makes no more difference than if you were spawned in some alien sea on Eridani! You are who you are <u>now</u> and who you will be tomorrow; the man and the child you were in the past are ghosts, spirits of the dead who merely grow restless from time to time. And some spirits, my friend, are best exorcised without mercy. Lay them to rest as an actor lays his past roles to rest, and look toward tomorrow, for all else is fallacy and illusion.

I cannot help but ask myself if it is love itself from which you are fleeing – love and the fear of losing it. I ask myself if there is an answer for you – or for any of us – or if you will continue to sift sand in vain among the stars forever, never finding your home and never returning to Terra, and never caring if we make love under watchful stars again. I pray I am wrong. I pray to nameless gods that you will not discover your Emerald Cities to be nothing more than green paint on crumbling ruins.

Forgive me, beloved, for I am hurt, and my greatest fear is that Time alone cannot cleanse these particular wounds. At first, the shock of being without you was so great that it made bravery an easy *mask to wear. But now that you have been among the cold starlight for a month (so pitifully short a time, isn't it?) and I have had those hours to consider the ironies which Fogg comprehends so well, I think the original disbelief has dissipated, and I have come to know that I have lost not only you, but a part of myself as well. Perhaps stated rather romantically, but such is not my intention. I speak literally, Raine, for I feel as if you have stolen some intangible part of me that is no less real than flesh or blood or bone. I cannot explain it, save to say that I am connected to you; our minds have known one another too intimately for me to simply forget; our thoughts have meshed too often to ever be completely sorted. And you have taken that with you – stolen that part of me which can neither be touched nor held nor even understood. Treat it kindly.*

Last week, out of frustration and a love which I can no longer contain, I booked passage to Lunaport, and had it not been for some medi-tech at the Nevada Launchport who happened to notice that the documents I was carrying were forged, I would be halfway to Altair by now. You have driven me to madness, Raine. You would have even driven me to death if I had not been discovered in my insane scheme to follow you. But you see, I learned that I would have had at least six weeks of life before some tiny virus could infect my blood, grow to maturity, and do enough damage to destroy me. And six weeks with you would be far preferable to the remainder of a lifetime without you.

At any rate, I did not succeed, and now I bear the tattoo on my hand of a fanatic who has attempted to leave Terra "despite medical contraindications." I have been branded as a lunatic who harbors a wish for death. The state psychiatrists who poked and prodded me at the launchport did not believe that love was valid enough cause for my irrational actions. Freudian bastards. If I had told them I was following my mother to Altair, perhaps they would have smiled and sent me on my way.

But again, I am sorry. And at the same time, not at all. If the beginning of this letter was written in anger, rest assured that it is also written in love – the ultimate freedom and the ultimate albatross. Two days ago, while attempting to convince myself that you were no more or less than any other Terran, I slept with a young *man whom I've known all my life. He is dark and beautiful and reminds me vaguely of you. And yet, despite whatever feelings of lust passed between us, the energy was not the same. He fucked like a god, but had no concept of how to make love with his thoughts. And such is the common curse of the majority of beautiful Terran males. Why did <u>you</u> have to be different?*

I tell you of this interlude not to anger you or arouse the worthless emotion of jealousy, but to let you understand that there is no other... and never can be. Before I was born, I thought of you. And after I am dust scattered upon these fields which no longer bear fruit, these thoughts will be no less intense. And in this bitter moment as the rockets belch fire into the night sky, I despise you for that!

Collette is going back to Lunaport, by the way. Permanently. She gives no explanation, other than to say there is something about space that has infected her blood (what a glorious choice of words!) Her eyes are brighter and more haunted than before, and her husband has agreed to the divorce. I shall miss her, and envy her her freedom. And also in this embittered moment, I despise her, too.

I am back in Florida now, and though there are certain changes, the atmosphere is always the same. My mother used to say that Time is kind to this place, that it walks more slowly through the willows and azaleas than through slums and ghettos of New York and Los Angeles. Perhaps she was correct in that irrational assumption. I have taken a small apartment until such time as I can assess my life, decide what to do next. The room where I am sitting as I write this overlooks absolutely nothing. However, when the sun is low on the horizon and the heat monkeys aren't so angry in the black and potted asphalt streets, I can walk to a place that is similar to places you and I used to walk.

There is a small forest nearby, and the palmettos are filled with roaches and spiders and innumerable life forms which spread themselves on the broad leaves close to dusk to feed upon one another without guilt. Terrans to the last. The pine trees are in bloom now, and one must be careful not to walk barefooted upon the spiny cones.

Last night, in spite of the street noise in the distance, I thought I heard something altogether miraculous. Two birds were going about the task of courtship high among the oaks, and I was certain that I picked out the cry of a redwing. I sat down among the fallen Spanish moss (and now I have chiggers and itches and fond memories), and contented myself to listen, comparing the sound in the trees to the sound recordings made before the War. Eventually, however, I discovered that my hopes had been In vain. It was nothing more than a mockingbird — a common mockingbird mimicking the lonely mating cry of an extinct species. And yet... should I believe that this ventriloquist was merely recalling that sound from its own racial memory... or should I allow myself the luxury of believing that it was mimicking a sound which no human has heard since the War? In short, I am wondering if some stubborn pair of redwings survived where the bomb's memory was short. Perhaps Man was not quite so efficient after all, in his attempt to obliterate life. Perhaps the survivors are at last coming out of their hiding place to face their old enemy once again. I hope we can be kinder this time... I hope we can be wiser.

I must go now. It is late here, and the whip-o-wills have been silent for hours. The old man who lives across the hall will be disturbed by my movements if I remain awake much longer. He paces the creaking wooden floors at night, and tends to his dying wife who is terrified of the roaches and long legged spiders which populate the toilet facilities after dark. He told me yesterday morning that he had once visited Altair — "when he was young" — and that the wildflowers and the rocks and the air were no different than here on Terra.

He is only forty six (biological years), yet he seems so very old. He says he too will die soon, and there are no stars in his eyes any longer, beloved. He is almost blind, and informs me sadly that he can no longer even see those dim points of light in the sky. He can only talk of being young now, for he will never live those glory days again.

And that is what frightens me, Raine. I do not want to become nothing more than a storehouse of anecdotes to be related to frightened children who happen by the apartments from time to time in search of a cure for their boredom. When I am old, I shall fall silent and selfish, for my memories shall belong to myself alone.

And, of course, to you.

Give Fogg my love, and tell him to be careful of things that go bump in the starry, starry night.

Forever... (or until we forget)
Crystal
Communications P8VEZ-Orlando.DYAZ

PS -I have decided to take one of those chances we were always wondering about – I have decided to see if it's possible to go home again, despite the words of the philosophers. Through luck – or perhaps through Fate, I discovered yesterday that the ranch is being sold. With the last of the money I had saved, I've put a down payment on the land (how odd it feels to be buying the one place on Earth which I've always felt was my home), and the old man who currently owns the place has accepted my terms. In some ways, I will be sad to leave the apartments, but in other ways I am pleased that I will never have to learn the fate of the old man and his wife. No doubt, the children will continue to come and the roaches and spiders will scarcely notice my absence. Wish me luck, beloved. And perhaps the Fates will be gentle enough to grant that one final request.

Go where you must; do what you must do; and think of Terra and of me once in awhile.

––––––––––

5th June, 2184
Crystal:

I am writing this before receiving your response to my former letter. I seem to know that you will not be eternally forgiving of my decision to leave Terra despite your kindly transmission of 12th May. Once the shock is gone and reality (such a dull gray demon) returns, I fear that your anger will surface – and rightfully so. But nonetheless, if I have learned only one thing through the time of my existence on Terra, it is that anger is perhaps the most healthy of all emotions. It purges the soul and can be an effective mask against the pain we are both feeling. I sense your thoughts even here – in another transport headed for a Regulan moon where Fogg and I will board the Sleeper ship for the Outerworlds. I know you are a reflection of my own mind at this moment; you are cold, frightened, alone and attempting to tell yourself that life and Reality should not be so cruel and indifferent.

And perhaps that is another of those radical ironies we have discussed so often in the past. Reality is an illogical master, beloved, but it is the only master we have. Some have called it God, some have labeled it Fate; but some have said that God is dead and Fate is nothing more than a series of coincidences linked together to form Reality. And Reality, then, is all there is. At times, I have considered those Terrans who populate the asylums and especially the inhabitants of the cemeteries to be fortunate souls indeed – for they alone are free of Reality. They do not adhere to its regulations; they are free to live their lives and think their thoughts in freedom and without repercussion.. For after all, who would dare to condemn the madmen for their madness? And the dead... theirs is another Reality altogether. Another type of freedom, a final repose in defiance of a universe that lives on without them... cooking hamburgers and tossing Frisbees and laughing and crying without their approval or disapproval.

I envy the dead, love... yet I am afraid to join them. And such is my curse – to be forced to accept Reality for what it is: master of all, lover of none, an indefinable word.

As to Regulus itself, Fogg and I discovered that there was nothing of value there despite the glamorous holos we have seen on Terra advertising the pale yellow seas and the clear amber skies. Apparently, travel brochures aren't very different anywhere in the galaxy. I recall a time in Earth's history when beautifully colored leaflets in bus stations presented New York City as a megalopolis of adventure, a Mecca for those seeking wealth, fame and excitement. In Reality (there's that

28

word again), one seems to notice the sterile gray asphalt streets steaming after an acid rain, the bums sleeping in narrow doorways, the bag ladies, the stench of overflowing sewers, and the overwhelming noise which finally blends into one single cry of remorse. The smiling faces seen so prominently in the travel brochures, those handsome men and beautiful women, are just an artist's concept of another reality. And the Statue of Liberty is a warden who smiles down on her prisoners and beckons more into the ranks.

In short, Regulus was much like what New York City was before the War came and mercifully destroyed it. The streets of Regii, (the launchport city where Fogg and I were staying) were cold and narrow; and the remnants of the last snowfall were piled high against the sides of anonymous red brick buildings. It makes me wonder if red bricks are the calling card of same mischievous universal demon — a sign that those who live inside those walls are forever doomed to loneliness and despair. Upon my return to Terra, we shall never set foot in a building which consists of red bricks and cold steel fire escapes.

Before the War, I once visited a young woman who lived in such a place. She told me that there was a hive mind in those tenements — that the woman who was an alcoholic and spent her nights puking in a filthy communal toilet was just as much a part of that hive mind as was the artist who lived on the twelfth floor and never touched alcohol or drugs. The alcoholic's midnight gagging was as much a part of that society as was the minor-keyed song of the poet who could not hold a steady job.

And I wondered then if all of Terra was a gigantic hive of related creatures who spend their lives in a vain quest to outgrow or outrun the pain, to overcome the grief, to simply survive and perpetuate the hive for posterity.

Fogg and I remained on Regulus for one solar week in a building that would have felt quite at home in some industrial city back on Earth. The black soot from the rockets had settled

29

without prejudice upon pagan churches and mortuaries and restaurants; and children were rarely seen in the streets. The children of Regulus play on the tops of tall buildings, and the most common accident is falling to one's death while chasing a ball that was thrown just a little too hard. There is, I suppose, that moment of unreality which is such a merciful part of any childhood — that moment when there is nothing else in existence save the ball one must catch in order to prevent The Other Side from scoring.

If I sound disheartened over my voyage thus far, perhaps I was expecting to leave Terra to discover those brave new worlds that early writers immortalized in their novels about the Joyous Wonders of Space. In truth, the sewers and skeletal trees against cold silver skies aren't much different on any world one might visit. And though the hue of the sky might vary slightly from planet to planet, the ultimate cause is pollution rather than magic.

Fogg, in one of his rare optimistic moods, pointed out that Regulus and Altair are simply too close to Terra – that the indifference and the nausea and the stark pain which is evident in every face one sees is merely a reflection from the Earth herself. He says the Outerworlds will be more fruitful, and that it is somewhere out there where we will discover our answers. I hope he is right, for I could not bear to think that the entire race of humanoid man is doomed to repeat Terra's mistakes on a million worlds throughout the galaxy. There must be a place somewhere which is an exception to that rule, beloved, and it is there that I am going.

One interesting thing is that those intelligent species which are not humanoid in appearance will have little or nothing to do with Terrans. While a lynxman from Criod IX might offer a passing gesture of kindness to a Regulan whore who has gone hungry for two days, he will deliberately cross to the opposite side of the street to avoid passing into the psychic aura field of a Terran. Are we that poisonous, love? Are we that utterly hopeless and contagious that even the

30

most alien of creatures can sense it? There is little difference between a Terran and a Regulan, yet the lynxmen and the Foriuns and the gaseous creatures with no faces or form who hover in line at the launchport can immediately discern which is which and react accordingly.

Yesterday, while waiting for our meal to be served in a filthy cafe on a side street of Regii, poor Fogg had the misfortune to brush against one of the Foriuns (they look something akin to an Irish Setter – with long sharp faces and intense blue eyes) who was seated at the next table. The Foriun flew into an uncontrollable rage – speaking in a language that consisted of a series of grunts, garbled moans and wounded cries – then fell silently across the table and lapsed into unconsciousness. All that from a simple and seemingly harmless accident. Fogg said that, for the instant his mind brushed the Foriun's, he thought himself finally cured of his humanity. Such discipline, such order, such tranquility... and such lack of purpose.

And the terrible thing, beloved, is that all the Foriun's discipline was forfeit – not only for the moment Fogg was in physical contact with him, but forever. It seems that our madnesses are indeed contagious – that our dreams and aspirations and fears and dark mental alleyways are deadly. The Foriun will live as an outcast among his own people for the rest of his life, by his own choice. And there will never again be tranquility within his tortured mind. It is, according to Fogg, as if the Foriun tasted the blood of all collective devils, or saw the Medusa of legends. I have attempted to explain to Fogg that the accident was not his fault, and though he seems to believe me on an intellectual level, I can feel the sadness reflected in deeper comers of his mind. In his soul, he tells me that he is ashamed to be a Terran.

This particular transport, in contrast to the *Dorsai,* is nearly deserted. Fogg and I have been assigned to the lowermost deck (perhaps an omen?), and he has been silently working on his novel since we left Regulus. He tells me with a certain degree of frustration that he is not satisfied with it – which leads me to believe he will make an excellent writer one day. Poor Fogg. How I wish he were not an empath sometimes. How I wish he could find someone who would make love to him rather than merely entertain him with the well-practiced motions of sex.

At any rate, this transport is relatively old as Terran spacecraft go, and I am convinced that the section we now inhabit was originally designed to transport bodies back to Terra after the Earth/Regulan conflict twenty years ago. The feelings of death are quite at home down here in the bowels of the ship, and there are no viewports. The dead have little need for scenic beauty. Six G-bunks are strapped to the dark green bulkhead, paint is chipping away from the cold walls, and some budding artist has scrawled crude drawings on the back of the main hatch. The graffiti, is most profound. It says, quite simply:

TERRANS GO HOME

Perhaps Fogg and I should take heed of that now, before we board the Sleeper ship and thrust ourselves even deeper into the belly of darkness.

Alas, I must close, for I feel the protest of the engines which marks our descent to Trellius – the largest of the Regulan moons. We will be ground-bound for approximately a day, and I shall digitize Fogg's novel during that time and send it along with this transmission. After that, beloved, I do not know precisely where we will go. Fogg intends to enter a state of productive meditation tonight, and perhaps he will gain some insight into our destination. If I am fortunate, he will merely smile (how rarely he does that these days), and say that there are no answers save those lies we manufacture for ourselves and that the sanest thing we can do is come home to Terra. More likely, however, his insanity and my own will take us on to the Outerworlds and beyond. I shall write again as soon as we awaken from the Cold Sleep and let you know of my whereabouts.

Most importantly, beloved, understand that I cannot help but think lonely thoughts. And happiness, though essential to existence, is not to be found so easily as it once was.

Wait for me... if you can.

Until...
Raine
Communications#71498878DEC

3rd June, 8 Trellius
PS — Trellius is populated by whores and pimps and fat green shopkeepers who would be most comfortable in red brick buildings back on Terra. The skeletal remains of a fated rocket lie exposed close to the main launchpad, and Fogg informs me that he will not strap into a G-bunk and allow himself to be injected with the Cold Sleep so long as that sight is visible. He tells me of the spirits who linger about the wreck — the transparent, invisible souls who perceive themselves to be asleep in some rocket bound for Lazali or Tremonol. He claims he can see the ghosts, beloved, and that they are angry and restless and displaced. He says that one among them is (was?) a Terran who is now trapped here and can never go back to Earth. Perhaps the philosopher was correct for all of us: *You can never go home again.*

Fogg says that the dead Terran was a child en route to an illegal adoption somewhere among the Outerworlds, and that the young boy will never again play baseball on a hot clay field on Earth or climb high into some secret tree loft with friends he left behind. The child, like so many of us, is property of the stars. And the saddest part of all is that that his spirit must remain forever here on Trellius — like some ghost in a Shakespeare play, doomed for a time to walk the night.

I cannot control the shivers I am experiencing, nor can I quell the lonely tears that fall when Fogg tells me of that Terran child. And sometimes, if I am sitting near the window which overlooks the launchpad, I think I see a morose figure pacing about the wreckage, carrying a small suitcase in one hand, and wearing a faded Yankees baseball cap that must certainly be a relic from before the War.

Forgive me, but you asked to hear of the children, and that child is the epitome of all that we are, were, and all that we will eventually become. The futility, the loss... and, of course, the irony. I cannot count the times when you were young that I lived in constant fear for your survival — the times when you would sneak out of your home late in the evening and walk unafraid to a black cypress lake that crawled with poisonous vipers.

I never completely understood your reasons, but neither did I need to understand you in order to love you. You later told me that you simply enjoyed tempting the Fates, but I suspect you were merely a child who did not yet know that Death is the intersect point of all Realities. At any rate, I loved you for that irrational fearlessness, and for your childlike innocence that kept harm away.

Here, at last, is a portion of Fogg's novel. He sends his love and his sorrow... and his hopes that we will be home again soon.

Always....
Raine

Raine was a magnificent, dark-eyed animal and a living enigma. I realized that from the moment I first saw him. It was perhaps five years before the War, and he was standing at the edge of an orange grove somewhere in the middle of Florida.

It must have been late in the spring, for honey bees were busy pollinating pale white orange blossoms, and the sticky sweet scent of impending summer lay heavy in humid air. Raine seemed to be looking for something or someone, and though it is possibly a farfetched and romantic notion, I personally believe he was waiting for Crystal even then, nearly a hundred years before she was conceived in her mother's womb. He was preoccupied and utterly distant, and I had no doubt he would remain completely oblivious to my presence as I watched him from afar.

His hair was somewhat lighter then than now, and shorter than the length to which it has grown since his departure from Terra. It was the shade of dark chocolate, and hung in wisps to his collar, giving him the appearance of some clean but untidy angel or devil, and making his eyes seem even blacker than they were. I could not help but admire the lean musculature of his body. Like a cat, he was, ready to stalk some unseen prey or simply lie down in the sand and allow the warm rays of sun to penetrate his olive skin. He could have been no more than 32 years of age as he stood there with his hands on his hips, staring into the rows and rows of dusty trees with their unripened fruit and gnarled, thorny limbs.

His eyes were so intense, so deep and rich and full of life that I caught myself fantasizing he had just stepped off some elaborate craft from another world (though Terra did not know of life on other worlds at that time) and that his mission was to save the Earth from itself with his beauty alone. He was, as I have said, *extraordinary*.

But Raine could no more have saved Terra from its impending War than he could have reached back in time twenty years to prevent the extinction of the whales or the construction of condos in what was once Central Park. He had neither the knowledge nor the drive to find that knowledge. His mind was property of the stars and love and romanticism – and nothing else had ever mattered or ever would.

I think it wise to point out that I was empathic even then. I was already deeply into Raine's mind without realizing it, and was seeing things from his perspective as much as from my own. Therefore, if at times my words tend to wander over seemingly unimportant or repetitious details, you must understand that there is some significance – if not to you or to myself, then to Raine or Crystal or to whomever I was reflecting at the time. As an empath, it is impossible to sort out what I am thinking and what someone else nearby is thinking, and I fear it was this shortcoming within myself which led to my original infatuation with Raine. I do not regret this, I merely state it for the record and with complete transparency.

Raine's mind was like a sponge then – a sponge that has become dried in the sun and will soak any moisture into itself. Even then, he was wandering about the face of Terra like some ancient nomad, even then he was lost and alone inside himself. But that fantastic mind was impossible to ignore or to escape — his search for answers, his quest for knowledge, his ability to ignore that same knowledge once he unearthed it. I was drawn into him from that moment, and eventually into those he loved or hated or passed in the night, and to this day I have no desire to be freed from his influence.

I loved him instantly.

He stood at the edge of the grove for a very long time — until the sun had started to set and the whip-o-wills were calling to one another from unseen vantage points high in the pines, and a few lonely crickets were conversing loudly on musical wings. Raine listened to them until well after dark, and his thoughts turned to a past lover — a young woman with whom he had been romantically involved in Arizona.

She had lived alone, Raine recalled, his thoughts easily slipping into my own mind. And he had happened upon her by nothing more than chance. I did not understand it then, but

Raine later explained to me that his first memories were of the desert where he had first met Aralin. Prior to that, there had been nothing to fill his memories, and it is those gaps for which he now searches. I hope he will not have to search forever.

It was in the winter when he first met Aralin, and winters were always beautiful in the desert. The dunes were quiet and still, the sand warm but not hot under his feet. Pale golden lizards seemed to glide over the dune sea like tiny lifeboats, oblivious to the expanse of the ocean in which they swam. Beyond the dunes, stark and barren mountains stretched skyward, their peaks and summits appearing randomly like broken teeth of some great dinosaur that had fallen on its back and ceased breathing forever. Closer, at the edge of the dunes, were the pale stone boulders which resembled nothing more than rock piles — so symmetrical they could have been carefully stacked and molded together by an intelligent entity who had been bored one day and had nothing better to do in the universe.

Raine seemed to think of his past lovers not so much by their physical appearance, but in images of where he had first encountered them, learned to know them, made love to them. He remembered not in dialogs, but in scenes and images and romanticism, and even then I thought it peculiar that any Terran could have so very much love and hope within himself.

The world was a busy place – a place that no longer had time for lovers and philosophers and mystics. I did not comprehend this at the time, nor do I think Raine himself understood it, but as the years continued on and he and I remained unchanged by Time, I came to know that an immortal does not measure the hours or the days or even the decades by the people who surround him, but by the very Earth itself – the only other thing with whom he will share eternity – the Earth and the mountains and the deserts and the sea and the dark void of Mother Space. All else is a spectral illusion composed of ghosts who will linger no more than an instant.

He thought of this desert with a certain fondness and a definite respect. He had been lost, it seemed, having left the main highway in order to rid his mind of the persistent thought which told him that he was not alone here, that his trip through these mysterious parts was not a unique one, and that thousands of other young men hitchhiked the same route every year. He possessed no knowledge of how he had come to be in the desert to begin with, nor where he had gotten the faded denim jeans or the soft white shirt on his back, nor precisely who he was. He possessed a name and nothing else other than the gnawing aggravation of knowing that his journey was of spectacular unimportance.

In that way, Raine could have been considered arrogant by someone who did not know him well, for he was obsessed with the desire to be unique, to do things no one else had conceived or attempted. He was a child – and that child had wandered away from the main highway, slept the night among the huge boulders which provided some scant shelter from the windstorm that came, first whispering and later shouting, through the dune sea. And when he had awakened the following morning, he came to realize that there really wasn't much difference between one huge, smooth boulder and another. The dunes had shifted and changed their faces like court jesters or actors in a play who portrayed more than one role.

He was hopelessly lost.

But in that displacement, Raine had experienced a definite twinge of joy and excitement.

It wasn't until two full days later, in the bright and almost painful glare of morning sunlight, that he saw the glint of metal somewhere in the rocky valley below the fallen dinosaurs. And while he had more than enough food and water to last another week, he felt drawn to the single house with its reflective metal dome mirroring the sun back at him as if in jest.

Aralin was perhaps the last thing he had expected to find living alone in a desert that could boast temperatures well over 120 degrees in the summer. Her skin was bronze suede from the last season's sun, and the soft brown tint of her eyes gave her the illusion of being something more than human. She was well-muscled from the difficult existence of the desert, and Raine could appreciate a woman's athletic strength as well as a sharp and uncompromising mind. In fact, he often found himself inexplicably drawn to the powerful women even more than those who could have passed for models or well-pampered wives of successful businessmen.

Perhaps Raine harbored a certain need to be vulnerable at times, to abandon the pose of male self-assuredness and discover himself safe in the arms and the mind of someone who was his equal. And, in admission of that need, it is possible that Raine was more honest with himself than most men would ever dare to be.

He stayed with Aralin for five years. I could see that clearly in his mind as he stood there in the oncoming darkness at the edge of a grove in central Florida. His skin had grown darker in the desert, his muscles had become more catlike and lithe, his shoulders slightly broader; his ability to love had deepened, and that great mysterious fire had never left his eyes.

But something had gone wrong somewhere in the desolation of the desert. The First Skirmish came – a seemingly unimportant battle in China concerning export rights of rice and paper fans. But it was the First Skirmish that would eventually grow into the War. No one knew it then, for the real War was still four years in our future. But the skirmishes and the international tension and treachery came closer to American soil – first in the Island Republic of Hawaii, then on Cuba, and finally moving into Long Island and Manhattan. At first no one knew precisely what was happening. It seemed that people just started getting sick –

colds and flu and childhood-type illnesses that didn't seem too serious at the time.

The irony, however, was that several Typhoid Mary's had been sent from non-allied countries in an attempt to diminish the population to the point where attack and eventual control would be simple. Those who didn't die immediately were too sick or crippled to fight, and this was years before the first actual battle ever happened. The jets took the diseases to every state, every county, every isolated township, and left a quarter of the population dead from mutated strains of common viruses.

Including Aralin. Despite her rugged beauty, despite her strength, despite Raine's love... she died, a casualty of a War not yet declared, not yet realized, not yet fought.

And Raine had found himself alone in the desert again, left to bury his memories in a shallow grave and mark Aralin's departure with stones and fragile wildflowers that would wither in the first cruel heat of the morning. He did not stay to see the sun rise. Instead, he found the railroad tracks and climbed wearily into an empty boxcar that would take him as far from the desert as he could go.

And now he stood at the edge of this grove, cursing love, swearing never to allow the emotion into his heart again, vowing to abandon love in order to abandon pain. He was purging himself as if in some ritual from his past, and I suddenly understood something very sad. He was tearing the last remnants of Aralin from his mind... or so he told himself.

But Raine would never be free of his love – not then, not now, not ever. Love was as much a part of Raine as salt was a part of the seas. It shown in his eyes, though he rarely looked directly at anyone for this reason after Aralin was gone. Terrans were too hungry for love, he realized, they would see the bright promise in those wide black eyes, and he would be doomed to repeat his own history.

He loved no one else until nearly a hundred years later, when the old curse he put upon himself must have lost some of its potency. There were, of course, casual interludes, an occasional embrace in the darkness, an act of animal passion to quell angry frustrations. But there was no real human love in Raine until much, much later.

I studied him carefully as he stood there, letting the darkness put its long black arms around him. He never knew I saw.

*

When the War came I lost sight of Raine for many years. I did not know if he had gone away, like so many others, to fight the hideous conflict, or if he had slipped into some untortured corner of the universe where Terran atrocities could not find him. I suspect the latter, though we never discussed the issue even when I finally found the courage to actually meet him. As I have mentioned, Raine did not measure time by people or interludes, but by the soil, the geography, the air.

And when the face of Terra was assaulted by bombs and fire and floods and tidal waves, perhaps he was afraid that he, too, would change, would begin to age, and would finally die. Not that Raine was particularly afraid of death, but he was not yet *ready* to die. By the time the War was in its fifth year and drawing close to its merciful end, he had started to fully realize that he was different from those with whom he shared the planet. If he permitted it, he discovered that he could read minds as easily as reading the back of a cereal box, and yet, there was something about this "gift" which completely unnerved and angered him. He did not wish to share the fears, the fading hopes and the shattered primal dreams of his fellow Terrans.

Perhaps it was this similarity between Raine and myself that drew us together once the War finally ended. Or maybe it was nothing more than cosmic fortune which delivered me back into South Florida two weeks after the last bomb had fallen from the sky and devastated the population of New York.

The bombs were such funny things. They killed without insight, without hindsight, without preamble, and without prejudice. And yet, they were sentient in some inexplicable way. They left the buildings, the subways, the dark and dismal tenements with their faded red bricks and skeletal fire escapes. The bombs killed the bag ladies and the whores and the wild dogs without discrimination, but left the bags and the whorehouses and the fire hydrants for the next generation.

New York City was transformed into a massive ghost town, its streets littered with corpses and baby carriages and ragged pipes spraying stagnant water into poisoned air. And the buildings overlooked it all, like some collection of unearthly sentinels who found the greatest humor in the altogether morbid situation.

The few people who were immune to the chemicals contained in the N-bombs took upon themselves the task of cleaning up the carnage, of telling themselves that The City would never fall, and that they would never ever leave it. Never. New York, New York. Forever New York.

They turned taxis into hearses and the East River into a gigantic cemetery where, hopefully, the swift currents would take the bodies – and the memories – far out to sea, where no one would be reminded that the War accomplished Absolutely Nothing.

Balance of power, balance of horror, balance of weapons. In the end, that's all it turned out to be. Neither side had superior weapons, each side merely possessed the *same* weapons in mass quantity. And once it became apparent that the only way to win this War was to bring out the nuclear arsenal – completely unrestricted – is when it stopped. Someone with a small thread of sanity got scared. Just like that. Apparently neither side wanted to be responsible for the total annihilation of life on Earth, so both major parties simply agreed to take joint credit for obliterating half the population and let it go at that. Period. No hard feelings. End of War. Shake hands and come out rebuilding for The Next Time.

No countries changed government, for in the confusion, no one seemed to have the presence of mind to start a revolution even in the smallest of dictatorships. No land was gained or lost. No major political figures lost their lives (for presidents, premiers, kings, queens and dictators were safe in the bosom on the sky, sailing their flying fortresses of War like ancient gods). And absolutely nothing-but-nothing changed.

Other than the fact that 5 billion people died. Some from radiation from close proximity to the N-bombs, some from the fire bombings in the initial skirmishes, some from starvation, some from ground fighting, and some from the easiest and most logical option of all: suicide.

Five billion people gone forever, the Earth a graveyard, and at least seventy nine species of animal life gone, including the lynx and the redwing blackbird and the common pigeon which shall nevermore defecate upon statues or store fronts. Gone. Half the United Stated and a third of Europe transformed to wasteland until the germs and radiation subsided to "acceptable levels". And nothing accomplished. No reason for War other than to prove that War was still in our nature, and perhaps to reduce the population to a more sane number. China still exported rice and paper fans and Americans and Europeans and Australians still ate their rice and fanned themselves on hot summer evenings.

And Raine's eyes were still just as hopeful and full of life as they'd ever been. He seemed unscathed, totally untouched and unaffected by the psychosis that had leveled San Francisco and turned the midwest into an extension of the Mojave desert. Either he had slept through the entire nasty affair, or he'd been precisely in the middle of it all and was now completely mad. I did not know which, but I was so grateful to see him – alive and apparently healthy – that I couldn't stop myself from watching him in secret once again.

As I have stated, he came to Florida after the War –

perhaps because the abundance of rains and winds there swept the poison from the land more quickly than would have been possible elsewhere or perhaps he was simply biding his time, waiting for Crystal to be born and grow and to reawaken the love that had been put to sleep in his mind.

I stared at him from my hiding place for a long time, at first attempting to decide if I myself were insane and merely imagining that this dark avatar had survived the War and was once again standing at the edge of the same orange grove where I had first seen him nearly seven years before. I owned a small house nearby, and it was my habit of taking walks through the skeletal trees whenever possible, so perhaps it was nothing more than coincidence which placed us both in close proximity once again.

I had left my home during the War and served as a medical volunteer, though my training was minimal, and I mainly assisted in the burials of the masses. I had fully expected to return to Florida to find my tiny house demolished – or worse, inhabited by Renegades – so perhaps the same miracle that caused Fate to overlook my home was the same miracle that brought Raine back to life as well.

It was summer, and the heat could have been responsible for visions, but I seemed to know instinctively that Raine had come back here for a reason. His eyes seemed so bright, so full of promise, so devoid of the pain that had reduced most men to candidates for the asylum. He started to walk, and for awhile I was content to follow, curious as to where a man like Raine would stop and rest for a moment.

He made his way through the rows of trees, not seeming to notice the thorny-fingered limbs that reached out to pluck at the long-sleeved black shirt he was wearing. He was totally oblivious to the heat, to the burning sands that surely must have left blisters on his bare feet. Even the rumble of thunder in angry black-faced clouds seemed to escape his notice as he kept walking and I kept following and we trudged on until nightfall.

At last, when the first drops of rain were purged from the sky, he found his destination. It was a small pond situated on the opposite side of the grove. On the far side of the pond, tall cypress trees stretched skyward in abundance, each swaying in a different direction as if they, too, were still confused about the War and did not know how to behave now that the world was half destroyed, but at peace.

He knelt by the water as I remained concealed just inside the last row of trees, and I thought for a moment that he was preparing to offer some prayer to whatever god had completely spared this place from destruction. Granted, the orange trees would be barren of fruit for decades, and it was a lonelier place without the flutter of the redwings and the serenade of crickets, but it was essentially untouched if one could suspend disbelief long enough. Raine stared down into the black cypress waters for a long time, kneeling as if in homage to magic. And then he sat down, curling his long legs underneath him and tossing the dilapidated backpack onto the ground behind him.

It was almost dark, but finally I was able to see what he was looking at. Hundreds of minnows were playing close to the edge of the pond, each one making a tiny ripple as it came to the surface and plucked at floating plankton. And Raine was utterly fascinated with this aspect of life which had gone on since the beginning of time. It was undisturbed life, which no one other than Raine had ever taken the time to notice in this particular pond. And in that, he was fulfilling his obsession. He was looking at anonymous life forms, his eyes alone were observing the muted colors on the tiny fins of the tiny fish who had lived all their lives there and would die there – perhaps never to be seen by human eyes again.

When the sun had completely dropped beneath a gold-crested cloudy horizon, and the rain had stopped falling from the sky and the world drifted into utter silence, that is when I first saw Raine. *Really* saw him. He lay back on the moist sand, using the tattered backpack for a pillow, as close to the water as he could get. He fixed his eyes on what few stars could be seen through the remaining thunderheads, and I couldn't help but know what he was thinking. His mind was open to me then – open to me and everything and nothing in particular – and I felt momentarily guilty for having followed this enigmatic creature to his private, secret place. Some things were born to be aloof, untouched and unknown, and Raine was the mightiest survivor of that breed. He was a dark and troubled stallion who had been banished from the wild herd, a specimen of perfection lacking only in companionship.

As he stared at the stars, I felt his mind slip open a little wider, and though the morally correct thing for me to do would have been to retreat, to pretend that I had merely experienced a post-War hallucination, I fell into him, into whatever strange ballad his thoughts were singing, and though I did not consciously will it, I became part of him that night.

Without speaking, without knowing it, his mind was whispering, conversing with whomever was lying by a pond on another world circling a star upon which only his eyes were affixed at that moment. He considered eternity and all the stopping points along the way, and his mind spiraled deeper into blackness. Eternity was somewhere in the void, he thought. Eternity was a tourist attraction in the furthest galaxy, where seedy carnies served up purple cotton candy and rode a shabby merry-go-round made of the skeletons of real unicorns and griffins and the bones of slain dragons.

I stopped breathing for an instant, and listened to the sounds of the night as I watched Raine watching the heavens. Somewhere atop a long-nettled pine, an owl was mourning the War's destruction in a melancholy voice that was contradictorily joyful. The minnows made loud popping noises as they devoured long-legged mosquitoes who had settled down to rest on the glassy pond; and close to my own ear, I detected the monotonous buzzing of some fat black insect who later alighted on my neck and began to feast. Food was scarce; I couldn't begrudge the hapless creature.

For what seemed like years, Raine simply lay there, his eyes locked on some invisible companion who did not exist. His thoughts were of the War and of the end of the War, and of the Wars yet to come. And of the loneliness that was temporary guardian over his soul. He pondered past lovers and past acquaintances and past sexual partners, and none had faces or eyes or bodies or personalities. They were only isolated moments when the emptiness had been a little further removed from his mind. They were ghosts of an alternate reality, and in that moment, Raine did not know who or even *why* he was. I felt a tear slip from his eye and nestle into the thick hair by his ear, and I tasted the salts of grief over everything, and yet over nothing he could have named.

And that is when I came to know I could no longer remain anonymous. I knew that Raine was someone dangerously like myself – someone who had lived too long and not long enough, and who would continue to live until all the answers fell neatly into place. I stepped out from my hiding place and walked forward as if entranced; and though he certainly must have heard my clumsy footsteps, he made no effort to turn his head or even glance to see if I was one of the Renegades – those poor bastards who had lost everything, including their minds, and lived only to kill and multiply the losses of those who remained marginally alive.

I do not believe Raine cared, I do not believe he would have moved if I had attempted to slit his throat or strangle him with the yellow bandana around my forehead. I stopped, standing mute at his feet for a long time.

"Hello," I said at last, surprised at how loud my voice sounded in this quiet place. I wondered if I had made the correct decision, or if, in fact, the decision had been fated in the cosmic charts of reality centuries ago. And yet, there is no proper nor improper manner by which to address oneself to a being such as Raine. One simply does or does not, and there is nothing more or less to it.

Still, he made no move. Instead, he merely closed his eyes and touched the ground beside him.

"Sit with me," he said momentarily, and I thought I had certainly been mistaken for someone else. After all, the War had just ended, and trust was a scarce commodity. I did not move.

And, after a time, he opened those dark eyes and turned them on me. Even in the darkness, there was no mistaking the expression which bespoke confusion and compassion and resignation and raw human love. Raine's eyes were filled with love – not for Man or even for me, but for the mystery and the danger of life itself. Love for the nights and the sunrises and sunsets yet to be.

For a moment, my thoughts returned to legends of vampires who mesmerized with a look; and were it not for his complete and utter beauty, Raine might well have been one of those mythical creatures. And his voice... I had never heard him speak until that moment, and I realized that I had not experienced the complete man. His voice meshed with his physical beauty so perfectly that I wondered if such a flawless being could be real in any sense of the word. Terra, after the War, was no place for gods.

But as I finally sat down, as close to his side as I dared, I discovered that the stillest of waters do indeed possess an infinite depth. I was compelled to look away.

"I... I have b-been w-watching y-you," I confessed, cursing the stammer of my childhood, but feeling a dangerous exhilaration in my statement.

He nodded, lips parting in a faint and informed smile. "I know," he whispered, turning his eyes skyward once again. "And what have you seen?" he wondered. "What have you learned?"

I swallowed with difficulty, realizing I had no answer that would not be a pure admission of my love for him — a love I wondered if he would understand. As an empath, I could not become a part of any relationship. That, I suppose, is my curse

48

for whatever sins I committed in previous lives. The feelings, the love and the hate and the moods of the other person would always be reflected, until I would eventually become lost and sacrifice whatever it is that I am or was or might one day become. I wanted a friend of the mind, a companion of thoughts, and Raine seemed to understand that instinctively as I noticed what appeared to be a moment of compassion cross his handsome features.

"No matter," he said when I did not immediately answer. "You need not have an explanation for your behavior." His smile grew. "That is, after all, one of the joys of being human, is it not?" He patted the ground, motioning me closer. "Do you have a name? Or are you some displaced spirit who has the unfortunate doom to travel this Earth?"

I knew by his light tone that he wasn't altogether serious.

After a moment, I leaned closer, resigning myself to his influence, almost hungry for the peculiar sensation of being drawn inside someone again — someone who, unlike the victims of the bombs, was not in pain, not dying, and apparently not embittered. As an empath, that mental union was inevitable.

I chanced a look at the creature who had so fascinated me secretly for years, then quickly lowered my eyes and looked at the stars' reflection in the still black cypress waters.

"M-my name is F-F-Fogg," I stuttered at last. "And as to whether I am a d-doomed spirit, perhaps I shall never know." Instantaneously, I felt the change beginning. If, before meeting Raine, I had spoken as a simpleton with a tendency to stammer, I knew those traits were receding. Instead, I began to speak as Raine might have spoken, to think as he might have thought – in a somewhat poetic manner which had deserted most Terrans centuries before. Poets had no place in the cities and the sewers and the planes carrying bombs, and Raine might well have been the last of his kind.

Of my former life, I have little memory. Like Raine, consciousness seems to have begun as an adult for me. I explained these similarities to him, astounding myself with words that began to flow from my mouth without stuttering interruption or even conscious volition. His presence was as a magnet, pulling forgotten memories from my mind. I told him of my past — which was really nothing more than dark shadows in the mind. I blurted out my infatuation with him, with his intellect, with his pure and unrivaled beauty. And I finally told him that I could not help but love one who seemed to be the epitome of all which love really is.

My love for him, I should point out, was not of a sexual nature. Rather, I loved Raine as one might cherish a priceless work of art or worship a golden idol. I treasured his thoughts, for they were poetry in a world which remembered only curses. They were clear and clean water in a radioactive desert. But the painfully embarrassing thing was that Raine had known all these things before I ever spilled them into that mysterious night. He had known, he told me, for years.

He smiled once again, sometime in the middle of the evening when the stars had started to travel to the other side of the sky. "And tell me, Fogg," he said in that cool velvet voice. "Tell me what you think of the War."

He asked it as casually as if he had been inquiring about the weather. For a moment, I felt the awkwardness return. I stammered, wordlessly, suddenly uncomfortable. I did not know where Raine had been during the conflict itself, and I had no desire to offend him by stating that I believed soldiers to be pawns and fools, only to discover that he had been a soldier. But I slowly made my decision.

"War is like a dance," I said, having no idea where my seemingly ridiculous statement would lead. "There is the courtship of bombs, the shifting of eyes back and forth as if asking permission to have the dance. And, finally, there is the pointless flailing of arms and legs, the ejaculation of violence. And the music which has no melody, yet seems to possess a frantic beat no one can ignore." I blushed, embarrassed at my peculiar description, but I could not stop. "And so the world

50

danced," I continued with an unfelt, nervous laugh. "We danced in the streets of San Francisco, in the corn fields of Iowa and in the basements and bomb shelters of Kansas City."

I shrugged, pretending indifference, suppressing the shiver of memory which slid along my spine. "And, at last, the music stopped. The drums have fallen silent, the musicians grew bored with tune, and all the dancers have gone to their coffin beds... at least for a time, until the dance begins again."

Raine looked at me strangely, then threw his head back on the pale white sand and laughed until I thought he would become sick. I did not, however, blame him for laughing. He was mad in that instant, and I had long ago grown accustomed to the sound of taunting laughter.

But after his amusement had subsided, he reached out and grasped my hand, gripping my fingers so tightly between his own that I thought he would break my wrist. But then he chuckled one last time, released me, and reached up to brush away the tears which had been squeezed from dark eyes during his outburst.

"Ah, dear Fogg," he said to me, his voice gentle and warm. "War is not a dance. It is a twisted confessional – a time when all the world becomes Catholic and falls to its knees and says to the firmament: 'These are my sins'."

He laughed again, but the sound had grown melancholy in the darkness. "And, like all human confessionals, it is doomed to be repeated, for Man cannot suppress his true nature. There is no final confession, Fogg, for there is no final sin." His eyes closed, then opened again. "And absolution is the greatest lie." He turned toward me, his eyes reflecting the light of Altair and Polaris and Eridani. "Absolution," he repeated with a very tender smile, "is a *lie*."

I looked at the sky, and for no particular reason, I knew Raine was right. There were only the stars and galaxies and meteorites and asteroids and nebulas and particles of insignificant dust. Whatever intelligence might be out there would surely be more concerned with its own survival than with ours. We hung on the edge of a galaxy, outcasts in a tenement known only as Terra. We were on our own.

We spoke little throughout the remainder of the night, but through the silence, I absorbed much of what Raine was. He was a vagabond and a sorcerer, a magician and a jester, an enigma and an answer. With his psychic abilities, I have little doubt that he alone could have prevented the bizarre conflict which had come to be known as the War. He could have opened the eyes of presidents and dictators and soldiers and made them understand that War is not one of the inherent rights of Man. And yet, he had apparently spent his time in some secluded corner of the globe – hungry for love, lonely for love, afraid of love. War and reality were the real illusions to Raine, for there was nothing of love in either.

When he finally did return to civilization (or what remained of it), it was to find the United States in a state of complete confusion. Individual states functioned as islands; and Central Government – though there weren't many high-ranking politicians left alive after the first N-bombs fell squarely on Washington – seemed inadequate to control rumors of secession. States which had been less damaged would have been quite content to fence themselves off from the throngs of survivors who were flocking to the few unpoisoned areas and uncontaminated cities which still remained standing. Eventually, California, Florida and Texas became independent "properties" of the States, allowing a controlled number of immigrants and turning the rest away. Governors became landlords, mayors became bosses of their cities, and the embarrassingly rich soon came to understand the meaning of pure communism. Land was divided as equally as possible, private property was confiscated to be sold, and one-room prefab houses were soon growing out of the sand and considered to be a luxury.

*

52

Raine and I spent the next eighteen years or more (one looses track of Time in a world which has abandoned the calendar and lives only for the moment of survival), talking of War and reality and confessionals and dances.

For awhile, shortly after the first intelligent extraterrestrial species was discovered living in a flophouse on Altair, I thought Raine would leave Terra altogether. I believed he would take a job for long enough to earn the fare to Altair – a world reputed to be paradise, a soothing ointment for War-weary eyes, a haven open to those with enough money to buy their way in. But Raine stayed, living with me in the tiny wooden house in Central Florida. He talked occasionally of "out there", of skies wider than the mind could conceive, of blackness between the stars, and he wondered how, in the midst of all that expanse and beauty, Man could still be afraid of the dark. It was, he once told me, no more threatening than the concept of being carried in a woman's womb. He would dream of floating as a disembodied thought through the void, and for awhile that was sufficient for him. He did not need to *go* to Altair. Or so he said. Terra had not yet given him his answers, his one true love, and he was determined to wait until those events transpired before moving out into the void.

The news of Altair, I should mention, came as somewhat of a surprise – for it had not been public knowledge that Man had even been attempting to continue his quest into the unknown. Perhaps Central Government had decided to keep the news quiet until such time as their secret seeds bore fruit. What with the War in full swing, starvation and disease running rampant, it is even possible that their decision was a wise one. In short, no one other than the president and those few technicians at NASA who were involved knew that four astronauts had been launched out into space nearly a year before the War ended. Perhaps, Raine speculated, even the kings and perpetrators of War had grown frightened; they had, in their fear, primed and readied the two men and women and had sent them "out there" in the hopes of somehow preserving a small segment of Mankind – our curse upon the universe.

The truth behind Raine's suspicion was never ascertained, but it would not have surprised me if such were the case. Man, it seems, is obsessed with the need to survive, to continue as a species, and at more than one point in the War, it seemed that leaving Man and his insanities behind was the only way for Man to continue.

According to the brief newscast which mercifully interrupted the War reports and the daily reruns of *Leave It To Beaver* and *Mayberry RFD*, the *USS Starbourne* had touched down on Altair, and had discovered intelligent humanoid species flourishing on the planet. The atmosphere of Altair, according to the astronauts' report, was cool and breathable; the technology was in an advanced but "temporarily arrested" state; and the Altairians themselves were a friendly and accommodating people who offered refuge to the survivors of our War.

Of course, by the time the transmission reached Terra, the War had been over for nearly seven years, so by the time Raine and I learned of the discovery of extraterrestrial intelligence, the four astronauts and two representatives of the Altairian Parliament were already halfway back to Earth.

The president addressed the public via radio and television, and even he seemed genuinely surprised that Man had finally accomplished something in space. Of course, this man in a three-piece suit who stood before the cameras spent the majority of his speech concentrating on the hope that technology would soon begin to boom again. There would be jobs for the jobless, homes for the homeless, hope for the hopeless and so on and on and on. He talked in political language and in unconvincing terms of eternal peace on Earth, and of mighty rockets that would be built to make mining and colonization possible "out there" on the habitable worlds of endless space.

Raine switched the vid off halfway through the speech

and walked out into the biting January morning air wearing only a faded T-shirt and thin jeans that had worn through at the knees. I did not know where he was going, nor what he intended to do, for his thoughts were shielded to me then. For the first time since our meeting in the night by the black magic pond, Raine became a stranger.

Something about the discovery of life on other worlds had shaken him to whatever foundation he had built his life upon, and I did not see him again for three weeks. By the time he did return, most of the president's self-serving promises had already been set into motion. The township near our home seemed to vanish as the men moved into the cities to take construction jobs with rocket manufacturers. For a time, I thought that Raine had joined them, had simply vanished into the slums of some city where he would sell the labor of his hands for passage away from Terra.

Being without him was perhaps the most enlightening – and painful – experience of my life. During the years we had spent together, I had grown accustomed to his moods, to his silences, to his infectious laughter, and to the private tears that would fall without apparent reason on nights when the stars were bright and the moon was dark and there were no sounds in the universe save our own breathing. I had grown accustomed to thinking as he thought, to living as he lived, and to being without the stutter and nervousness which had been my companions for as far into history as I could remember.

During the three weeks of his absence, I grew to understand that I was utterly displaced without him. I began to stammer curses at the television when some sub-cretin character would take a pie in the face, or when some brave galactic hero would save the galaxy with a plastic studio prop. I became embittered and cold without Raine; and for the time he was gone I lost sight of love altogether, which led me to realize that Raine *was* my love. Through him, I *could* love – safely, without fear of becoming lost in the mind of another man or woman. I was, perhaps, a parasite, though I like to tell myself that our relation was a symbiotic one. I could feel Raine's love without the necessity of responding to it, and there was a balance in that which was both secure and rewarding.

While Raine was away, however, there were no warm thoughts in the evening, no images of men and women walking together, no thoughts of passionate lovers entangled on a round bed covered with black silk sheets. My thoughts grew sterile and difficult during Raine's absence, and perhaps I should have learned something from that. Perhaps I should have noticed that I was little more than a mirror whenever Raine was near; I was a reflection of his mind, his thoughts, his very soul. Perhaps, I told myself one bitter evening, he was merely using me to groom himself.

I realized and understood the fallacy of such a thought, but I could not control it. I recalled things he had said. I remembered him telling me that, like couples who had been married for too long, we had even started to look alike. He did not seem to find this objectionable, and yet I asked myself if I were stealing from him, sucking his very essence into myself and guarding it as I would have guarded an endangered species. Perhaps I should have left that small two room house sometime while he was gone, left him to be the person he was destined to be.

But I was a prisoner. Without bars on the windows, without locks on the doors, I was the ultimate prisoner. And so was Raine. Somehow we were bound together – like two pieces of a puzzle that had been glued together until there could be no separation.

When he finally returned, unshaven and hungry, he said nothing of his whereabouts of the past three weeks. I suspect he had gone into the City to stare at the ruins which were coming to life, to think of the ruins of other worlds, or to stare with those black eyes at the children who were cursed to play in the streets and share their bed with rats.

I had learned that the "Technology Race" had already begun; the drive to reach Altair en masse began almost immediately. Terrans were starved for a world that was not poisoned, for a world that didn't yet possess the weapons to wage War. And Raine had often stated that he would be the first to go "out there" if the opportunity arose. But for some reason he never discussed with me, he did not choose to go that year. He merely walked back into the living room late one February afternoon, gave me one of those hopeful smiles and asked quite sincerely why it was that neither he nor I had aged in the years we had known one another.

Raine had an uncanny ability for posing questions which had no logical answer; and I told him, trying not to stutter, that I did not know.

But he shook his head, sat down on a straight-backed wooden chair at the kitchen table, and began to pick absently at the worn cuff of his sleeve. "The reason we have not aged, my beloved Fogg," he finally said in a melancholy voice, "is that the world and those who presume to run it do not yet know that we are here."

I stared at him, blinked, and wondered what in all the undiscovered worlds he was talking about.

"We were born out of time," he clarified, sensing my confusion. He looked up at me, dark eyes raw with a love he could no longer control – a love that compelled him to search for it, believe in it when no one else would. "We were somehow created before our creation was destined to be. And time, while attempting to battle wars and produce babies and keep rain from falling too often in the desert, has simply forgotten about us."

I sat down by his side, listening to the creak of the chair beneath me. It was certainly riddled with termites who now had fat round bellies, and would laugh their silent laugh when the timbers gave way. They were biding their time, just as Raine was.

"Do you believe that?" I asked, almost startling the silence which had crept in to hear Raine speak.

He laid his head down on the table, weary from whatever journey he had undertaken, and laughed just once. It was a cold and lonely sound. "No, Fogg," he whispered. "I do not."

I felt something akin to sadness come into the room to keep the silence company, yet I made no effort to chase it away. "What, then?" I wondered aloud. "What *do* you believe? What do you want?"

Raine did not look up. "I want something that does not and cannot exist," he murmured, and buried his head a little further under his arm. "I want to have no wants."

I sat there for a very long time, simply admiring the shiny hair which fell across his face as if to shield those mystical eyes from a cruel reality. After a time, I rose, went into the bedroom and found a blanket that was not too full of holes. Draping it about his trembling shoulders, I pretended not to notice that he was crying in his sleep. For Altair. For Terra. And all the darkness in between.

He slipped a little deeper into sleep as I touched him and tried to draw his pain away. In his dreams, he was sharing passion with some imagined woman who had never been born, and who would not exist for another thirty years. It would be another fifteen years before Raine would even see her for the first time, and five more following that before he would find a way to introduce himself. For, despite his easy rapport with me, Raine was an unusually reserved and private person.

I shielded myself as best I could from his stray dream fragments, not wanting to intrude on a paradise that could safely exist only in the sanctuary of a perfectly ordered yet absolutely troubled mind.

*

Raine's dreams and expectations and frustrations continued for another four and a half decades; and when I came to believe he had abandoned his frantic search for love is when he eventually discovered it.

He had taken a job at a small bar in what remained of the settlement near our house, and spent his evenings dispensing drinks and courtesy to the rocket men who were contemplating an affair, to the whores who were contemplating God, to the outcasts who were contemplating suicide, and to the wino who was contemplating nothing more than his half empty bottle. Raine was well suited to the job – yet he did not particularly need to work in order to survive. The fields near our house provided ample food, and the local co-op was always pleased to receive our fresh corn in exchange for more seeds, and to provide used blankets and other household necessities in exchange for the fresh strawberries and fattened cantaloupes which Raine seemed to coax out of the ground with ease.

I used to watch him toiling over a plant that wasn't entirely healthy, nursing it back to health, and finally plucking the rewards it provided some months later. The ground was rich and fertile despite the War, and after Raine had spent so much time learning to grow things in the harsh terrain of Aralin's desert, this work was simple to him. We always had a variety of greens, lettuce, onions, potatoes and even an occasional watermelon. And so, we had always lived in comfort despite our occupations as members of The Unemployed, and after a time I came to understand that I had not missed eating the flesh of animals (which only real money could buy). Meat became as prized as gold had once been, and in a country where the economy had collapsed, it was not uncommon to see shabbily dressed farmers leading cattle to what had come to be known as "flesh banks". Rustling, black market sales of meat, and a somewhat unorthodox breed of cowboys were resurrected, and history began its course again.

Raine's job at the bar, however, was taken primarily out of boredom. He had grown weary of the silence, of the darkened silhouette of the City in the distance at night, and he told me that one must eventually resign oneself to discover whether Man has ever changed or ever will. And, according to Raine, the only way to make that discovery was to mingle with one's peers when they were most vulnerable. The only way to get inside a person was to know them after they had left their jobs in the city, after they had laid aside their slide rules and picks and shovels and all the equipment that enslaved them to humanity.

I visited the bar only once, and found that the unshielded thoughts of those prisoners of life were too rampant, too violent, too passionate, too beautiful and too raw. And yet. Raine's thoughts, images from his mind would come to me in the night – when he was at work and I was sitting on the back porch of the house watching the stars fall from the sky in brilliant green and white flashes.

The building that housed The Round Table was situated on the edge of Highway 41 – a road once populated by leviathan trucks and speeding tourists who had come "Down South" to vacation in winter. But now that the majority of private vehicles had stopped functioning and repairs were too expensive, the road was traveled mainly by local youths in solar-powered contraptions that greatly resembled golf carts, and by hitchhikers who all seemed to wear the same haunted expression of one who has looked into the face of a Medusa or a god.

Raine thought of the hitchhikers often – of those men and women who would wander into the bar, slump wearily at the counter, and drink without speaking until the doors were closed and the flickering neon sign was extinguished at 5 each morning. Raine would watch them leave then, back into the streets which were their only property, walking toward some unknown destination which, quite probably, no longer existed. The hitchhikers were running, Raine knew, and their footsteps would gradually fade into the fog until he would find himself wondering if they had ever been there at all.

He once jokingly said to me that there were doorways

along the highway – doorways which only the hitchhikers could see. These doors, Raine said, were just like any other – except for the fact that they were not connected to any building or structure. They simply stood there in the darkness, only in the night, and each one led to a different point in time. He smiled as he spoke of the doors, and whispered something about the hitchhikers, wishing them God's speed to Neverland.

But for the most part, Raine contented himself to converse with the inhabitants of the settlement – the fat old man who came in every Thursday night and cried huge round tears into his merlot because his young wife had taken another lover, stating that she could not tolerate writhing pointlessly beneath the soiled sheets with an obese relic. And Raine talked with the young wife of the fat old man when she came in every Friday evening, proudly boasting of her fair-haired lover whom no one had ever seen, and who was the pilot of a star shuttle, and whom Raine told me did not exist, but was merely an extension of her lonely fantasies.

All these things I saw in Raine's thoughts, felt in his mind, experienced as if I myself had been there, pouring drink after drink for the prisoners of the depression that always results from awareness of their terminal mortality.

One evening late in April, however, it seemed as if everything came in on Raine quite suddenly. He was too close to the emotions, too near to the pain and despair of the bar, too close to the insanity or the balance or something utterly opposite of what he himself was. The local wino had lapsed into fitful unconsciousness in one dark and smoky corner of the room, and the line of farmers and businessmen and winners and losers had transformed into nothing more than a conglomeration of eyes with no faces. Construction workers chuckled over the latest flaw in the design of the 511 Starshuttle, and proceeded to take bets on how many flights the new rocket could make before it would implode in space.

The front doors of the bar were closed, holding the

madness within, but the back exit stood open, a faint breeze carrying the scent of jasmine in to momentarily obliterate the stench of cheap wine and spilled beer and stale smoke from somebody's homegrown weed. The breeze seemed to envelope Raine, singling him out amidst all those faces, hypnotizing him for a fraction of an instant as some oily serpent might mesmerize its prey before the attack.

The breeze, the serpent-wind *knew* Raine.

I do not know if this is fact or merely one of Raine's poetic thoughts, but what is important is that there was some trace of magic in that wind. It brought back a time before the War when jasmine and lilac had grown in abundance, and when people very much like the patrons of The Round Table would spend their Friday evenings at home in front of the vid. It came into the bar like a genie uncorked from a dangerous bottle, a wind from the past, a breeze that had been suspended in some secret corner of time for decades since the War had ended.

And yet, it also came through the back door like some under-aged youth who knew he could not stay long before being discovered.

When it chose to leave by the same door through which it had entered, it took Raine with it. He looked up from where he had been pouring a draft beer for the bedraggled man who attempted to grow pole beans and summer squash at the farm down the road, and simply sat the half full mug aside. His eyes must certainly have been bright that night, for though it is possible for me to relate everything which Raine felt, thought or did, it is not entirely possible for me to relate to you the depth of those eyes. He seldom looked at himself in a mirror, for the years had proven that there were no changes from one morning or one decade to the next. I saw things through those magnificent black windows, and that was enough.

He stared at the back door for a moment, his mind growing more and more removed from the clatter of beer mugs and the whine of depressed conversation. Through the open door, he could see the overflowing garbage cans and the skin and bones tomcat who frequented them each night. And yet, Raine was looking beyond those things as he removed the bartender's apron and walked like a man entranced through the wood frame door. If any of the patrons noticed him leave, they merely passed it off to one of his silent moods, and said nothing.

The owner of the bar slipped quietly into Raine's position, and time continued.

Once outside, Raine sat down on the concrete stoop, staring out toward the empty darkness behind the bar. Since The Round Table faced the road, there was very little to see behind it. A few banana trees which had long forgotten how to bear fruit still waved in the humid night air, and one lonely palm fanned itself with leaves that had turned brown from the drought. The grass had grown tall despite the lack of rain, and somewhere in the distance, he could hear the gentle whisper of water kissing an invisible lake shore.

Overhead, the stars were painfully white, like a million curious eyes that had come out to watch a man chase a breeze that had come from nowhere and disappeared back into it, a wicked siren known for leading men to their doom.

He sat there for what seemed like hours, his thoughts returning to the desert and Aralin and to the almost forgotten emotions of love and companionship. In the years Raine and I had spent together, he had taken perhaps five lovers, though none had lasted longer than a week, and he had not spoken of them in other than vague and lonely words. He said that they were there for a time, put there to hold for a moment in order to amuse some unseen god, and that when they were gone it was as if they had never existed at all. He was gentle with them for their time, but once that time was exhausted he put them aside like old clothes in a trunk and closed a door on them for forever.

I did not envy them.

There was a time, however, when Raine lost his gentleness and his compassion. I do not know all the details, for his thoughts were shielded to me for months following the incident. The only thing I am certain of is that the normal sensual and sexual drives contained in any man or woman were kept prisoner too long in Raine and that the woman who thought it humorous to tease him with her beauty paid a somewhat violent price.

He thought of her as he sat there. For what reason, I am not certain, though perhaps there was some certain scent in the air, some particular feel of the wind on his flesh that brought the past in alignment with the present.

Without ever having met this woman, I hated her as I have never before or since hated another living creature. The most I could discern from Raine's tortured mind – and this much taken while he slept (forgive me, Raine) was that she was of extraordinary beauty and cunning. And Raine, being an overly romantic and sensual being forever in search of love, was compelled to respond to that beauty and to the advances she openly offered one evening at the bar.

She talked of passion and soul-warmth, of fire in the heart and fever in the soul which could be alleviated by lovemaking and certain illegal substances induced directly into the bloodstream before sexual contact. She smiled at Raine while he was vulnerable, and told him of her travels to Lunaport and Altair IV – and she whispered of strange new methods of sexual union, and peculiar places on Terra where the mind was totally open to impulse, totally absorbing of love. She said she could take Raine to one of these places – and for some reason – perhaps his own desperate need to find love – he believed her.

After taking him to her flat, however, and offering him wine and warmth and the promise of bright red lust, she became the ultimate gamester, leading him through the motions, tantalizing him with words which were lies, finally refusing to consummate those lies. She told him there was no love in all the universe, that love and passion were fantasies, and that promises were only lies. She told him that one must learn to reject one's own drives. She tried to destroy Raine's ability to love, his ability to make love with such conviction and beauty, and he could not forgive her when he discovered that there were no creatures on Altair who thrived on love, that there were no love merchant drugs, and that she had used him for nothing more than her own petty amusement.

I am altogether certain Raine was drugged with one of those illegal substances reputed to increase the drive of passion and irresponsibility – a substance that destroys all reason and awakens the ancient lizard brain that knows only of taking what it wants with no regard for the consequences to self or others. I have told him of my suspicion, yet he will not accept even that as an excuse for his final action. The remainder becomes a blur of scarred images – struggling and resistance and rejection and violent rutting.

She was Renegade – a survivor of the War who had lost her mind, her balance, her reason for living, and was driven to obliterate those things in every other soul with whom she came into contact. She told Raine there was no love, and he was compelled to deny it – both physically and mentally. He was compelled to disprove her, and claimed her body angrily, with an ironic passion that was love and hate combined, validation and simultaneous negation of all she had said and done. And he took her mind telepathically – something she had not anticipated – filling her with images of love she would never know, completion she would never experience.

And yet, despite the unwarranted provocation and his own drug-induced response, he considered himself dangerous for months. He would not eat, would not speak, could barely even think. His mind sought the only refuge it knew – solitude inside itself.

It is true that Raine could have had any man or woman he desired. Indeed, the patrons of The Round Table often spent their evenings attempting to discover some way to invite him to their flats, yet he remained celibate and alone following the episode with the Renegade woman.

Raine thought of her again as he sat there on the stoop of the bar, feeling a breeze (but not that same breeze) dry the thin film of sweat on his chest. His shirt was unbuttoned, long sleeves rolled up to the elbows, and he probably looked extremely exotic to the town whore as she floated around the room boasting of how quickly she had made her last john come to fulfillment. Raine did not see her.

It had been over five years since the incident with the Renegade, and he could not banish those images from his thoughts. They lingered like angry spirits, and though he cursed at them and pleaded with them, they would not leave him alone. He wanted to love again, to hold a woman close and feel her breath warm against his neck as he joined to her. He wanted to taste true passion and eroticism and let *those* forbidden feelings lead him back to love, back to Terra before the War, back... *home*.

And yet, some stray thought whispered in his ear, telling him that love was lost to Terra forever. Telling him that love, like the daisies and the redwings, had succumbed forever and was gone.

But after a time, the drone of the bar began to intrude once again. The wino had regained consciousness and believed himself to be in the depths of legendary Hell. The two farmers who were twin brothers and liked nothing more than a practical joke were taking turns playing the role of Satan, telling the wino that there was no booze in Hades, and that the women had no genitals. They threatened him with rape by the lower demons, and watched his red face turn pale under the dim lights of the bar. The whore had joined in, attempting to pass herself off as an angel of the lord by gliding about the room with her breasts bared and her arms outspread as if to fly. She promised him relief and release and sexual pleasures – and told him that her breasts were fountains of holy whiskey.

Raine glanced over his shoulder at the madhouse, and for

one of those moments which suspends itself outside reality, he thought he understood something extremely sad.

This is all that remains of Terra now, he thought to himself. *The bars and the anonymous faces in them. The judgment day has come, and this is certainly Armageddon. Whatever good there once was in Man has vanished... and all that remains are madmen.*

That's all Terra had ever been... or ever will be.

Before the War was no different than after the War, and just as soon as Man's memory had started to dim, a new generation would learn the ways of War as well. The people in the bar were just amusing themselves while they waited.

It was as Raine had said to me that first night we met: *'There is no final confession, for there is no final sin... and absolution is a lie'.* Man's racial memory could never be long enough, and once the diseases and the immediate aches of War were gone, the dead Warriors would become larger-than-life heroes whom future generations would worship.

But the ultimate fallacy, Raine realized in the enlightened moment out of time, was that new generations did not wish to merely pay homage to heroes of the past. Each new generation must have its *own* heroes, its *own* Warriors, its *own* gods. Apollo died and Christ was born. Christ died and Hitler was born. Hitler died and the Bomb was born. And when all the Bombs had fallen and were silent...

The firmament would surely laugh at that – at the constant struggle Man maintained with his ancestors – the drive to produce the greatest warriors, the final conflict, the definitive god who would not desert them.

Raine watched the drunken whore and the suddenly sober wino, and thought for a moment that he should intervene, that he should attempt to somehow help the poor man who lived at the bottom of a cheap green bottle. Instead, he simply glanced back at the night sky and blinked the image away. What difference, after all, would his intervention in a small town brawl make a thousand years in the future? And, for that matter, what difference would it have made in that single moment? It would not cause the stars to fall from the sky, would not bring the redwings back, would not alter one single molecule in the memory of the universe.

He watched the sky and tried not to listen to the horrified shrieks of the wino, and his ears gradually attuned themselves to something else entirely. Something was walking down by the lake which he could not see. The footsteps were light and quick, and for an instant he thought perhaps one of the few remaining wild deer had come to visit the water and drink its fill in the dark when hunters were drunk and unruly children were tucked neatly into bed. And yet, as he listened more carefully, there was a voice as well as footsteps. A female voice – a voice he had been waiting to hear since his beloved Aralin had succumbed to an unnamed disease in an unnamed desert nearly a century before.

He became spellbound, with the wind holding him still and mute, listening to the voice that had no face or form in the blackness. It spoke softly, calling to something, and the footsteps gradually became slower until they ceased altogether. And that's when the voice stopped, too – leaving Raine to think himself mad, to believe he had finally slipped and fallen over the precarious cliff of sanity. But after a few moments, the sound came again, and though the voice was too far away for Raine to discern what was said, it took on a soothing, comforting tone.

He rose from the stoop, not realizing that he'd been holding his breath, and walked very slowly toward the source. The grass was moist from an early dew, and the scent of the lake lay heavy in the air with its musk and fish and deep, damp secrets. He stopped behind the banana trees and chanced a look toward the water. And there, standing just at the edge of a black lake which reflected the stars, was Crystal. Her back was to Raine, but it suddenly became clear what she had been doing. In her arms, she held the scrawny faded orange tomcat who had survived for years on nothing more than stale toast and rotting scraps from The Round Table.

Apparently, Raine thought, this woman who was no more than a child had been pursuing the cat for quite some time, calling to it, finally comforting it when at last it allowed itself to be picked up.

For a single moment, Raine felt the lost emotion flutter through his mind. In its terror, in its near starvation, the animal had come to her, abandoning fear and all instinct and placing its survival in the hands of another living creature. And Raine wanted very much to be that animal – not so much to be in this woman-child's arms, but to have the trust to do what the cat had done: to have the ability to set aside mistrust and anger and all the things that labeled him as Terran.

When the silhouette finally turned around, Raine was careful to remain concealed behind the tiny banana tree, but he continued to watch, seeing her through the darkness on that black night when The Round Table had gone insane and the rest of the world was quiet, and not even the hitchhikers had come around with their wild and staring eyes.

Her hair was long and golden and completely straight. It fell below her shoulder blades in back, a striking contrast to the rich tan of her skin. Her eyes seemed light, and though Raine could not discern their color, he would later discover them to be the same deep shade of green as the leaves of his treasured strawberry plants. And yet, the painful thing Raine observed was that she could have been no more than fifteen years of age. Had she been older, Raine might have gone to her in that moment, spoken to her in some poetic manner, and lost himself in the abyss of love without so much as a second thought.

She wore dark pants and a loose-fitting blouse which was cut low in the back and buttoned in the front, and she remained utterly oblivious to Raine as he watched her in silent reverence. Finally, clutching her newly found companion and wrapping the folds of the shirt around him as if to shield him from nonexistent cold, she simply turned and disappeared back into the darkness at the edge of the lake, leaving Raine alone and anonymous and hopelessly infatuated.

Perhaps it was nothing more than the scent of that breeze which had drifted into the bar and the madness of the people inside that caused him to love her from that moment forward. Perhaps it was nothing more than coincidence that of all nights, he had chosen that one to walk away from his job and contemplate the past. But when she finally passed beyond his range of sight, he turned back toward the bar and smiled for no particular reason. She had come out into the night – a black place populated by Renegades and madmen and romantics – apparently unafraid. Just to retrieve a starving animal.

And yet... she was no more than a child.

As Raine walked back into The Round Table with just a whisper of a wind plucking at the long strands of his hair, he realized something. Time had no real meaning for him, and for once he was grateful for that reprieve. He glanced out the back door one last time as he began refilling empty beer mugs and listening to the wino tell the story of heaven and hell.

The drunken man slumped awkwardly across the counter, his grizzled face suddenly seeming young and beautiful to Raine.

Raine looked at the back door, at the stars glowing low on the horizon, and thought of a girl growing into a woman.

He would wait.

*

When he came home that evening – or more precisely, when he slipped through the screen door at four in the morning like a man sleepwalking – he came into the bedroom, sat down heavily on the edge of our small bed and stared out the window for a long time without speaking. I could hear his heavy sighs, his heartbeat, the thrum of reawakened blood coursing through his veins.

"Fogg," he said, not needing to look in my direction to know I was awake. "Fogg... I believe there may yet be hope for this wretched ball of radioactive sludge upon which we attempt to live."

I smiled to myself in the dark womb of itchy blankets, for I could not help but be amused. Raine's joy was so tremendous that it melted into me as dye soaking into virgin fabric. For a moment, I was so dizzy that I could not move, did not trust myself to speak. For sixty years that I was certain of, and only the gods know how many more before that, Raine had been an ultimately sad creature. Yet now, in the course of a single mystical evening, he was transformed into some gloriously happy being. Maybe it was nothing more than my own imagination, but I thought for an instant that there was an actual glow surrounding him. Or perhaps that was the power which made Raine unique among all other Terrans.

He could channel his love so easily, so naturally. And since love, like all emotions, is nothing more than a series of changes in brain wave patterns and an increase of certain biochemical energies, it is possible that I was merely observing some natural occurrence. People fell in love with Raine on a daily basis — from the lonely patrons of The Round Table, to the girl at the co-op, to the young man who would stop by the gardens early in the morning to watch Raine work. They all worshipped him with such fervor, such passion, such ignorance of the creature who truly lived behind those black and ageless eyes.

But the fact is that they were *compelled* to love him. His aura drew love out of people just as the sun caused plants to turn their leaves skyward and flourish. Yet in his kind and polite and gentle way, Raine had rejected all of them.

But as he sat there staring out the window and watching the sky begin to lighten and turn silver-blue, I knew he had finally encountered one being he would not be able to reject.

"Tell me of this creature," I prompted at last, stumbling upon my words in my sleepy stupor.

He smiled — that wistful, almost painful smile of his, and just kept staring at the dew on the cantaloupes in the garden.

"She is a fantasy, my dearest friend," he said to me at last.

"For certainly she cannot exist in reality on a world such as Terra has become." He shook his head, his hair blowing almost sadly in the morning breeze which had parted the curtains and come through the window for a brief visit. "I have created her from my own thoughts, Fogg, and now she walks this Earth alone." And what he said next was barely a whisper, as if he feared to speak the confession aloud. "And... I cannot help but love her."

At first, I found myself wondering if Raine had finally broken his own rule, and had sipped some stale brew until his mind was lethargic with liquor.

"A hitchhiker?" I wondered, not trusting myself to open my mind fully to his thoughts and images and dreams. Usually, that was how Raine and I spoke – through a series of mental pictures and emotions which circumvented the need for awkward verbal expression and the inadequacy of words. But this time – when I was already so certain that his love was genuine – I think he needed that awkwardness, the clumsiness of real speech that was such a burden and such a joy to Terrans. He needed, quite simply, to be something less than a god for a moment, he needed to become fully human, even if for just an instant.

"No, not a hitchhiker, dear Fogg," he murmured, eyes closing as he let the picture of Crystal drift into his mind. "Definitely not one of those sad-faced sirens who would lure her victims upon the rocks. No... not a hitchhiker and not a barroom soul... and not yet even a woman."

The smile departed from his face as his eyes opened and he turned to look at me, leaving me suddenly uncomfortable. I felt he was peering into me, probing whatever it is man defines as the immortal Terran soul. It was as if he somehow needed my approval to love again, to search for love, to be compassionate. I squirmed uneasily and tried not to shiver under his scrutiny. His eyes were darker than I had ever seen them, seeming to reflect the indigo blackness which lives between galaxies. Yet they were also filled with love... and the

72

fear of it.

And perhaps there is some significance to that after all. Perhaps love is the darkest, deepest shade of black Terrans can perceive, for it is the presence of all other emotions, just as white is the presence of all pigmentations. Love is the maroon of passion, the pale gray of melancholy, the green of fertility, the yellow of happiness, the muted brown shades of jealousy, the cold silver of fear.

He carefully explained to me what he had seen that night, stopping occasionally to laugh at himself for his frivolous and utterly romantic choice of words. But what came through more clearly than the description of Crystal, her mannerisms (which Raine made up as he went along) and her personality, was the fact that Raine had started to believe he had somehow transformed energy into matter to create this image of perfection. Whether he genuinely believed this or was merely enhancing reality as all lovers inevitably do, I shall never know.

In truth, when I was finally able to open my mind to the images contained in Raine's thoughts, I perceived Crystal (that is what he named her; her real name, he learned years later, was actually Willow Harland) was possessed of no more or less physical beauty than any other young woman. In Raine's mind, I saw a female Terran with pale hair tied back from a slightly oval face. I saw green eyes behind long lashes. I saw a smile and felt a tenderness, heard a laugh and tasted a tear, heard a silence and a sorrow, a joy and a series of unanswered questions which fill the mind of any child. Physically, she was sturdy, with powerful muscles developed while training horses on a nearby ranch, and tanned skin from long and silent walks in azure forests. I caught the fading scent of freshly-mown hay — for Raine found more joy in the clean scent of the fields than in rare hybrid roses or perfume. In essence, he was seeing her through the blind eyes of a lover – for though she was an attractive young woman, she was not extraordinarily beautiful on the exterior. (Forgive me, Crystal, but I must attempt to make this account an honest one.)

But perhaps Raine was seeing more than Terran eyes can detect – even the eyes of an infatuated romantic. Perhaps he was seeing into her mind even then – on the morning after the night before, when he had watched her chasing a starving tomcat under pale starlight. It is possible that Raine's telepathic nature reached out to her, creeping into her thoughts and matching them to his own, and that there was never a decision in the matter so far as Crystal was concerned.

It is not that Raine would have forced her to act against her will. Yet because his search for love had been thus far futile, perhaps he would have reconsidered the depth of his moral conviction at that. Without his own knowledge or volition, like a child with a gun who did not know how to use it, it is within the realm of possibility that Raine summoned Crystal's love even then. He was already her prisoner as she would become his, and the bars were slammed shut on both of them simultaneously.

"What do you intend to do, my friend?" I asked of him as the sky began turning morning orange and a few clouds hurried across the horizon. "Will you speak to her? And, for that matter," I cautioned, "can you be certain that she is not already betrothed to another?"

His smile returned, lingering like dew on the leaves, and he shook his head as he returned his attention to the window. "There can be no other for her," he stated without hesitation and without a single gram of sanity. "And it is only a matter of beloved time before she recognizes that fact."

Perhaps my first impression of Raine had indeed been correct. He was a vampire who would mesmerize his victim into love just as he had mesmerized me. But instead of draining the life from them, he would fill them with his energy, his bright and hopeful thoughts, his beautiful silences. He would one day draw her to him and claim her soul.

I could not help but envy her any more than I could help but love her.

74

If Raine was a dark and mysterious being who felt more at home during a black night among the stars than on any sun-streaked beach, then Crystal was his equal. Raine had taken to watching her from secret places near her home – which, he discovered, was less than a mile from The Round Table and less than two miles from our own modest dwelling. And though he would occasionally express his feelings of guilt over observing her in secret, he would in the same breath tell me that she had surely been forged from his own thoughts, his own beliefs, his own quest for love. Raine grew to believe that this woman had been neatly placed in his path that night by the same mystical force which others might have dismissed as nothing more than coincidence. He perceived that she was a lost soul who had been born out of her true time – just as he claimed that he and I were of that same melancholy breed. And he lamented – countless times – the fact that she was only fifteen. And though she was mature due to the harsh existence Terra now demanded, she was hardly old enough to understand love, much less vow to share it with any one being forever. He told me quite sadly that she had to live before he could take her, that she had to experience reality before he could alter it for her.

He learned of her life through observance and painstaking research, even going so far as to call the school she attended, pretending to be her father (who, he learned rather embarrassingly from a suspicious school secretary, had been dead for years). He hung up the comcode phone immediately and vowed to be more cautious, discovering her likes and dislikes and idiosyncrasies from merely watching her. Occasionally, he would slip into her thoughts from afar – an action for which he chastised himself, but an action he seemed unable to control. And sometimes, he would even sift through the discarded papers in a trash bin outside her house. He learned that she, too, was lonely for the stars, and that her dreams centered around one day going to a thousand nameless worlds in a search of nothing in particular, just the joy of the search itself.

Perhaps it was then that Raine imagined himself to be some lost crewmember of an extraterrestrial mission that had gone awry, or perhaps this woman's longings touched something in Raine that had been lost to him. Perhaps she reawakened his need to search for the ultimate truth of Terra: her origins, her seemingly inbuilt compulsion to destroy herself.

And so he continued to watch Crystal, to study her moods and appreciate her simple beauty and marvel at her psychic pull on him for the next five years. He went to The Round Table each evening and told the businessmen and the whores and once told a Transport captain that his love wore faded jeans and dreamed of pale white stars, and did not even know that he existed. The bar's patrons grew accustomed to Raine's easy laughter, to the casual and poetic manner in which he spoke of love – a luxury so many of them had lost somewhere in the past.

He told of his sorrow when he had watched her fall in and out of love with another man. He spoke of his regret when she had finally married the scoundrel, but the relief returned to his eyes when he told of how she lad later discovered that her new husband had no real love to return to her. Raine spoke of how she had weathered the divorce and had returned to her mother's ranch in the country where she tended the horses and watered the fields and only rarely went into the City. He drank one glass of wine and told the bar's patrons of Crystal's midnight walks – of how she would slip quietly into the evening and stroll through the trees and pay no attention to the reality of snakes or Renegades. She was protected, Raine said. And she simply walked within the darkness, imagining that she was trekking through the forests of some alien world, on a world unspoiled by Terrans – a world which existed only

76

in the safe finity of her own mind.

But it wasn't until one October evening when skull-faced jack o'lanterns were scowling brightly from The Round Table's front windows in homage to some ghoulish holiday that Raine found the first answer to his long series of questions. He had been talking to the whore when the wino aroused himself from his stupor, strolled over to the bar, and grinned in Raine's direction, displaying badly rotted teeth and a tongue that had paled from too much cheap whiskey.

"So what're ya waitin' for?" he stuttered to Raine's astonishment. "This woman o'yours ain't gonna live forever, ya know, and if ya got the big brass balls ya were born with, I says you should tell this lady just how much you likes her."

The whore walked away then, rolling her eyes in disgust. Love did not exist in five-dollar-a-night flophouses.

Raine stared at the wino, then turned to look out the back door, where the garbage cans were full again, and there was no faded orange tomcat scrounging for scraps. He thought of a warm room, a warm bed with a quilted spread, and the cat now fattened and content, sleeping at his mistress's feet.

"But how does one approach someone one has never even met before?" Raine asked of the wino, who suddenly seemed to be the wisest man on the face of Terra. "How is it possible to-"

And the wino fell forward across the bar, collapsing into wheezing fits of sound which might have been laughter, might have been tears.

"Ya just does it, mate," he decided in a rough whisper that reeked of stale wine. "Ya just does it – or ya spend the rest of yer life livin' in a bottle because ya doesn't have the nerve. And ya wonder and ya get drunk so ya won't have to wonder what it would've been like if ya *had* had the nerve." His red eyes seemed bright to Raine, bright with experience and pain and a raw, unnurtured love Raine wasn't aware that winos could feel.

"After all," the old man continued, slapping a wrinkled

77

hand down across the bar to punctuate his statement, "she ain't a'gonna live forever... and neither are you."

His eyes studied Raine as if there might be some doubt, but he continued. "In a few years, somebody's bound to push the button again, and then you'll never have to wonder about nothin' again." He laughed once more, an oddly morose sound which overpowered the whine of the jukebox and the mumble of meaningless conversation "And if ya don't," he said through tight lips, "then you'll have nothin' to even be sorry for when the bombs start to fall. Nothin' to remember, nothin' to care about... no one to say goodbye to..."

Raine stood dumbfounded for a very long time after the old man had lapsed into silence. Then, with hands that struggled not to tremble, he poured the wino a drink, removed the bartender's apron, and quietly walked out of The Round Table for the last time

*

Raine walked slowly through the night, becoming part of it, listening to the owls and the dew on the grass and the stars talking among themselves. His thoughts turned to autumn mist, and after he had found his way to Crystal's house he leaned heavily against one of the thick-barked pines by the cypress lake and slid to the ground, not caring that the grass was cold and wet and not noticing some startled snake slither away from its hole at the base of the tree.

It is entirely possible that he was reflecting Crystal's mind even in that moment – and in the moment when he finally decided to leave Terra in search of his answers and hers – for Raine had never mentioned to me any urgent desire to leave Mother Earth before. It was a poisoned womb, but nonetheless ironically safe.

But as he sat there in the damp darkness, watching the stars doing nothing out of the ordinary and the rockets from Canaveral struggling to achieve orbit, something changed inside Raine.

He slipped for a single instant into someone else — into the skin and bones and marrow of a man he had never known before — but a man who had perhaps once been a piece of himself. The stars became nothing more than expanding gases in the void, the rockets chemically propelled projectiles. The grass beneath his feet was nothing more than cellular groupings painted green with chlorophyll. Love was a word with no meaning, for he was a child enslaved in a place where feeling was forbidden from the moment of birth. And he himself was merely a biological form with slightly more intelligence than the owls and the snakes and the so-called "lower life forms" with whom he shared the planet.

There was a coldness and an emptiness, but there was also total (albeit sterile) comprehension of all things. He could have explained precisely why gravity functioned as it did, he could have told me how many alternate dimensions would fit on the head of a pin, he could have explained legends. But he was incapable of comprehending the one thing which held all those tiny microcosms together: love.

He had lost his love for a moment, had lost his understanding of it, his need for it, had lost everything except the sterility of independent thought.

For that lost moment in which he became someone else, Raine forgot precisely why he had come to rest at the base of the thick-barked tree. He knew only that he was a creature capable of higher reasoning, but incapable of initiating or sustaining a true relationship. But the sadness in that recognition snapped him back to reality, shaking him with such ferocity that he found himself once again filled with a series of emotions, overflowing with hope and joy, for he had finally made his decision. He would talk to Crystal, for what did he really have to lose?

He took barely a moment to analyze what had happened to him, what had caused him to become momentarily lost inside his own mind, groping to comprehend a part of himself he had never witnessed before. Instead, he told himself that she would fill the empty places, leaving light in the darkness, creating memories where there were none before.

But he glanced at the stars one last time, and felt a shiver of anticipation go crawling ominously up his back. Perhaps that was why he was drawn to her – perhaps she was something more than human, something that would always be capable of love, something that had been spawned on a world far less cruel than Terra. Some men had often wondered if their old gods were bred in another stellar sea, and Raine found himself asking if Crystal had been the ancient mother of all of them.

He was, as I have said, hopelessly infatuated.

With a sigh of relief that had been held inside for the five years since he had first seen her behind The Round Table, Raine closed his eyes. She was old enough now. She had lived, and his wait would soon be over. He would go to her in the morning, talk with her, and take her reality down a different road.

He closed his eyes and let time walk slowly through the night.

*

Crystal came out of the old wood frame house which was home to termites and spiders and other unseen vermin who lived deep within the shaky beams and rafters. She glanced at it once, silhouetted against the late morning sky, and wondered how it stood upright in the middle of such a raging invisible war. Her mother, who now lived upstate, was always talking of selling the ranch and allowing Crystal to move to the City, but there were no buyers for the property, and the idea of relocating an entire lifetime's collection of furniture and breakables and memories was more talk than it would ever be action.

Raine knew that Crystal did not belong in the cities. The

soot of the rockets and the stench of clogged sewers and the explosion of Renegade shotguns in the night would bury the spirit that made her unique. As she walked along the path that would lead to the barn down by the lake, Raine slipped behind a pine tree and watched. He moved into her mind without directing it, without consciously wanting it... without being able to stop himself.

She thought of the coming of winter with a certain degree of sadness, for the thick St Augustine grass would turn brown and the mockingbirds would disappear from the orange trees, and the township would close its heavy wooden doors to wait for summer. And yet, there was also a longing for cooler temperatures, for those mornings when fragile icicles would hang from the loft of the barn like transparent knives, when the rockets would shine red against the silver sky, when the stars would be brighter on crisp December evenings.

Raine read her thoughts with as little difficulty as he had read her lonely writing which had been designated to the trash bins for the past five years. She thought in seasons and landmarks, in seascapes and changing colors, in shades of light and dark... but never in faces. And in that, Raine knew he had indeed discovered a kindred soul — someone who marked the passage of time by the ripening of fruit on the trees, observed the death of a friend by how long the flowers remained fresh upon the grave, someone who dreamed of future lovers and did not think of past acquaintances at all.

On that morning, she was wearing white pants which laced up in the front and back, and had once been known as sailor's jeans. Her shirt was a full-sleeved pullover made of a soft yellow fabric which gave her the illusion of a trapeze artist, though Raine did not know why he found that image such an exciting one; and her long hair had been tied back with a single gold clip until only a few strands were falling in unruly fashion to frame her face.

In one hand she carried a well worn leather bridle with snaffle bit which swung with a carefree motion as she walked.

In her other hand was a tuft of alfalfa hay, and under one arm she held an antique Australian stock saddle and faded lamb's wool riding pad. She thought of a world where there were high hedges made of lavender leaves, and horses jumped freely in less-than-Earth gravity. She thought of flying free in the void and making love to the darkness at night.

And Raine was forced to pull back from her mind.

The tack jingled with the sound of bells as she moved, and he thought of the wind chimes in Aralin's desert before the War. He recalled the cold tinkle of metal upon metal, and the scent of hot boulders and eternal summer. Crystal was, in many ways, like Aralin, but at the same time she was completely different. Aralin had been dark-haired and mysterious, but Crystal was light of coloring and far more perplexing of mind than Aralin had been even in her moodiest of times.

As she reached the barn and unlocked the stall, she began to fasten the tack to the dappled Arabian mare.

Raine made his move then, wondering why sanity suddenly seemed like the ultimate human fallacy.

*

He stepped out from his hiding place and made his way through the citrus trees which were already spilling fruit onto the ground. And though he had learned to move with a stealth and grace befitting the most dignified of cats, he could not help walking a little faster and clumsier than normal, and before he realized precisely what he was doing, he had stumbled into the open breezeway of the barn and leaned heavily against the stall – less than ten feet from the object of his affections.

She was bent at the knees, tying the cinch, and Raine realized in a sudden moment of horror that he had not given one single thought to what he was going to say. He stood there, short of breath for no particular reason, utterly terrified, until she looked up, meeting his confused expression.

Whatever it was he had expected from her, it had not been what happened. She merely smiled after controlling a small gasp of surprise, and rose to her feet with a quickness that would have matched his own. And for the first time in his life, Raine lost his poetry, lost his grace, lost his mind. It should be pointed out that although he had been studying Crystal in secret for years, he had never been closer to her than anonymity would allow. She had never seen him to his knowledge, she did not know that he existed, and quite probably, he thought, she did not care. She looked at him as one might look at some new species of amoeba under a microscope – studying him, judging him, wary of him, finally accepting him and mentally cataloguing him for future reference.

"You lost?" she inquired in a voice that was melodious and exactly as Raine remembered it from that night when he had first seen her chasing after a stray cat.

He blinked, stared at her, and managed to shake his head, wondering why in all the worlds he had taken the advice of a wino.

"No," he stammered at last. "I...." And his voice fell into embarrassed silence as she dropped the reins over the railing of the stall and took a step forward, her brows narrowing with curiosity.

What she saw was something she had never seen before, for although Crystal had known many men and loved a few, she had never seen – at such close range – a being so beautiful as Raine in such an obvious state of misery. He seemed frightened and perhaps even Renegade, leaning there against the stall of a barn on the first day of November.

"Well?" she encouraged with a gentle smile. "If you're not lost, then what're you doing here?" She inclined her head around the barn, at the bales of molded hay and the rafters that were decorated with elaborate cobwebs, at the tractors and rakes and shovels and rolls of barbed wire stacked haphazardly in one corner.

Raine swallowed with difficulty, and even from where I was still lying in bed back at our own house, I could feel his fear – the fear of rejection, the danger of being turned down by one whom he had come to cherish in secret. It was perhaps no different than in the times before the War – when young men and women would create fantasies involving movie stars – fantasies of being loved, how their idol would behave, what type of person they truly were. And then, upon actually seeing that idol in a crowd, having their eyes lock for the briefest of moments... with no recognition, no concern, no love.

Perhaps Raine had created that type of fantasy with Crystal – set her upon some pedestal above the Earth, and thought she would simply love him from the first second their eyes met in a crowd of faces. And yet, she only stared at him as if he was quite irrefutably mad.

"I wanted to talk to you," he managed at last, his voice sounding like that of a stranger as it came to me two miles away. "I... have been watching you for a long time." His eyes lowered, and he felt as a man in a confessional, confiding his darkest sins to one who would mercifully absolve him. "Please – hear me out?"

He could easily read her thoughts even then, even through the haze of his own fear, and it was not difficult to know what she was thinking.

She took another step closer, studying him, and simply nodded and perhaps that is what plunged Raine even more deeply into love. If she had refused, or if a string of curses had erupted from her mouth, perhaps he would have realized that his affection for her had been nothing more than a self-deluding fantasy. But in the innocence of her nod, perhaps she doomed herself – and Raine – to what eventually transpired.

"All right." she said, stroking the horse's rump fondly, then brushing the loose Florida sand from her knees with the other hand. She smiled again, and I saw her clearly for the first time as her mind opened and Raine seemed to flow inside her.

She looked at Raine with something that might have been the beginnings of affection even then, for she could not help but be curious about a man who had just confessed his darkest of all possible transgressions in a world where privacy was the most treasured of intangible things. She quickly crossed to the gate of the stall, opened it, and stepped through to stand less than three feet from him; and immediately, she knew she had indeed found something quite like herself. His aura was black – but not the evil which so many magicians had feared since Time itself began. Instead, it was the same shade of black as the shiny scales on a sunning Indigo Racer. It was the black of the void between the stars; it was the black of velvet and songs in E-minor and the waters on the lake on nights when there was no moon. It was soft black, and warm with colors that retain heat.

And all he could do was stand there, staring back at her with those wide eyes which promised the universe itself for nothing more than a casual asking.

She leaned against the stall next to him, and together they gazed at the mare who was outfitted for riding, but who was now standing alone in her stall, marveling at the curiosity of humans.

"So you've been watching me," she said with a faint little laugh that was somehow melancholy. "Would I be too presumptuous to ask why? And for how long?"

Raine closed his eyes. "As to why... I cannot answer, at least not truthfully, for I do not know," he said, managing to school his voice back to its usual level of self-assuredness. "And as to Time... it has been five years" He looked at her then, and a very faint smile came to his lips. "Do you remember a certain faded orange tomcat who once lived near The Round Table?"

She nodded, still staring through the open-ended stall and not meeting his gaze. It was several moments before she responded. "I learned something from him." She paused, her thoughts turning sad and lonely. "Some things are better off wild, untamed."

Raine asked no further questions, for it was obvious by the melancholy tune in her thoughts that the treasured animal had not survived... and he did not wish to exhume morose memories on a November morning when the air smelled of fruit that had been too long on the trees, and the faint feeling of a new winter drifted into the barn on each breeze.

She stood there for a long time, thinking of nothing other than tomcats and wild things and a man who had been watching her for five years with for no logical reason. And at last, she turned, met his eyes once again, and smiled.

"Come up to the house," she said, feeling no threat from him. "It's been awhile since I've had anyone to talk to – and you seem like you might be a good listener."

Raine blinked back the blindness which suddenly overcame him, but before he could respond, she had already started walking back along the sandy path, leaving him no choice but to follow.

*

Once inside the small house, she led the way through unopened cardboard boxes and antique furniture to the living room, where she sank down onto a sofa that seemed to open up and swallow her entirely. She motioned Raine into an old chair, and smiled with genuine amusement when he sat down gingerly on the edge.

"Sorry about the mess," she apologized, glancing around the room, "but ever since dad died, mom never bothered to clean the place up." She grinned. "And I'm not much of a domestic-type person, so... " Her voice trailed off and her thoughts ran deep once again.

"Who are you?" she asked at last, green eyes reflecting the light coming through the roll-out windows which were covered with dust and hadn't been cleaned since long before the War.

"My name is Raine," he replied with a gentle smile. "And though I know that it is not your real name, I have come to call you Crystal."

She laughed warmly once again, and shook her head in amusement as she unclipped the gold barrette and her hair fell across her shoulders. It was not every day that some romantic stepped out from behind a pine tree and told one that one's name was not what it really was.

"Well," she sighed, kicking at a plastic rug-runner that covered the faded red carpet, "I have to admit I like that a lot better than my real name." She shook the mane of hair back from her face. "Think I'll keep it," she decided impetuously. "If you don't have any objection, that is."

Raine's eyes widened with surprise. "I have no objections at all," he said quietly, studying the room in which he found himself. He shifted uncomfortably, for he did not really know how to go about the art of courtship. "Forgive me, but I was wondering if you might enjoy going to the launchport one evening and watching the ships depart for Lunaport."

Crystal stared at the madman with mild disbelief, and let her mind slip open a little wider. For a reason she could not immediately pinpoint, there was something decidedly different about Raine – he was not entirely normal, not at all like other men on Terra. He was naive and perhaps innocent, and she experienced a measurable degree of warm satisfaction in that.

"Sure," she agreed, "why not?" She paused, and a cloud of sadness seemed to pass in front of her eyes. "Maybe I'm imagining this whole conversation, but it sounds like a good idea right now – since the launchport is as close to space as I'll ever get"

Raine took a mental step backward, and spilled the truth before he realized what he was saying. "But it was my understanding that you wished to join one of the shuttle crews," he stammered out. "I thought-"

She waved his argument aside with a gesture of her hand and a dark laugh. "Yeah," she said, not bothering to inquire as to how he had availed himself of that information; it didn't seem to matter. "But what you want and what you *get* out of life are usually two very different things."

Raine looked at her for a long time, then opened himself to the sensation of sadness that seemed to be coming from this woman he had loved for five years, whom he had idolized, whom he had placed above the wildflowers and the beauty of the lands that had not been touched by the hand of War.

"It's really nicely ironic," she continued amidst the sudden midday silence. "But when I went down to Canaveral to take the prelims for the training, the medics found out that I'm one of those who can't leave Terra ."

She laughed again, but even I could feel her bitterness two miles away. "It's called Negative Genetic Immunity – which means, in layman's terms, that I'd be susceptible to any little alien virus that was crawling around in one of those transports. Hell, I can't even go to Lunaport because of the aliens out there. Even the ones who aren't sick are carriers of one thing or another."

Raine's brows narrowed, and he found himself wishing he were a doctor, a research biologist, an immunologist... anything more useful than the incurable romantic. "But you are safe here – on Earth, I mean," he presumed.

"Yeah, as long as I stay on Terra, where the immunity fields are theoretically locked into the atmosphere, I'm as safe as anyone else." She shrugged, as if attempting to convey an air of indifference she certainly did not feel. "But if I ever go out there – away from this ball of rock – then it's only a matter of a few days before I'd get sick.

"And yet," Raine surmised, "that is what you wish to do – leave Terra."

Her eyes sparkled with the irony. "Wouldn't *any* sane person?" She looked around, at the tiny living room, at the faded red carpet she could not afford to replace, at the dirt on the windows and the flowers blooming along the path that led to the barn. "Once you've seen it all, there isn't much else to do, is there?"

Raine leaned forward and was silent for a long time, for he understood all too well what she was saying. Terra was one world among billions, and after the War, jobs were limited, travel was strictly regulated, and one did not know from one moment to the next when the next war would begin. Any sane person *would* leave Terra... to the offworld colonies where jobs were plentiful and War was not a weekly game show on the vid. Any sane person would leave a world that had grown old and stagnant and full of death and cancer.

"But you are so very young," Raine said with a degree of sadness. "There must certainly be things you have not seen, things here which could interest you." *Someone you could love.* He stopped himself before saying it. Just thinking it, feeling it, needing it and wanting it. "You are *so* very young," he repeated fervently. "You have not seen the snow on the mountains of Alaska; you have not tasted fresh wine from an unknown vineyard in the West; you have not felt the spray of the ocean on your face-"

She reached across the distance which separated them to grasp Raine's hand. He gazed at their entwined fingers, and tried to understand why she had done it. Her skin was smooth, her hand strong, and a warmth and inner vitality emanated from her touch.

"I haven't done all those things personally," she agreed, squeezing his hand with genuine affection, "but plenty of other Terrans *have* – and it wouldn't be any different for me." Her brows narrowed as she looked into Raine's dark eyes. "Don't you see?" she continued in a painful whisper. "It's all the same; *we* are all the same. And if one Terran has seen the Grand Canyon or the streets of New York or the ruins of Tokyo, then we've *all* seen it."

She laughed once again, that tender and melancholy

laugh which moved Raine so deeply. "Nothing new under the sun," she whispered. "Isn't that what it's called? We're an old planet – or at least as old as we need to be for things to get dull. And with very few exceptions, none of us will ever see something or do something that hasn't been said or thought or done before."

She inclined her head to the window without taking her eyes from Raine's face. "That's why the stars are so goddamned important. There's new *life* out there, new blood, new thoughts and new faces." She paused, and when she spoke again, her voice was a study in wonder and despair. "And... haven't you ever wondered why none of those other races seem to come to Earth other than on layovers and transport fuck-ups?"

Raine shook his head, not knowing what else to do or say. He had, it seemed, selected the one woman who could think in parallel lines and concentric circles at the same time. She could rip the foundations out from under the meaning of life, and feel no sense of guilt or remorse in doing it. And he could not help but love her for that. So many Terrans had dedicated their lives to speaking kindly of the Earth and its creatures, but this woman made no effort to mask reality with pretty pink flowers and rosy perfume. The stench of Terra was the stench of rotting corpses in a battlefield; covering them with lies and kind epitaphs would not cause them to stink any less.

"The aliens don't come to Terra," Crystal continued, "because they're afraid of becoming exactly what *we've* become. They're scared to death of our minds, our thoughts... our stagnation." She pushed the hair back from her face and leaned closer, her voice lowering to a fervent whisper. "They're afraid of buying a picture postcard of New York, taking it back to Altair or wherever they're from, just to have some politician there decide that the slums are the most beautiful thing he's ever seen, They're afraid of taking a piece of us with them — and I can't blame them for that!"

She held Raine's hand more tightly, and closed her eyes as

if in disbelief of her own bitterness. "Haven't you ever heard the old saying that Centauri II is just a little bit like heaven was supposed to be?" She didn't wait for an answer. "Hell, Centauri II won't let Terrans land there even under emergency situations. They've never had a war, never had plagues or starvation, and they'd like to keep it that way. We're like a disease, Raine! And the longer we stay here, the more diseased we become." She fell silent for a moment, and when she spoke again her tone was gentler, kinder, sadder. "That's why I wanted to train for the shuttles – to get *away* from Hell and never look back."

Raine was quiet as he realized that he'd heard very little of what had just been said. Instead, he had *felt* it, deep in his mind, transferred through the warmth of her hand. He had felt the sadness, the frustration, the anger and the depression of being a prisoner. And he felt, more deeply than all the rest, the need for something intangible — changes, answers, mysteries. They were no more or less prominent than they had ever been, and yet to see his own innermost desires reflected in the mind of a woman he had come to love left him astounded and wonderfully bewildered.

He held her hand more tightly, marveling at the trust she must certainly have had to invite him here when Renegades were everywhere, and she herself had stated that some things were better off wild and untamed.

"I, too, have always felt a certain pull of space," Raine confessed almost to himself, only then recognizing the truth in his statement. He *had* felt the pull, that much is true. And perhaps it was only in that moment that he realized what had been compelling him. He looked out the window, and despite the fact that the sun was high overhead and the sky was painted a pale iridescent blue, he thought of the stars, and of how they were always there. "I have come to feel that there must surely be a reason for all of this – a reason for man's wars and his hatred, and even his...." *Love.* Again he stopped himself. "I have thought there must be an answer – *one single answer* – to why we have spent the majority of our history in a frantic attempt to destroy one another."

For surely, Raine understood in the silent regions of his mind, the first men who had slithered out of some primal sea and evolved and grew to maturity had not intended it to be that way. Surely, they had dreamt of warmth and security and a house in the suburbs with a white picket fence and children who would take their place when their time on Earth was done. They could not have envisioned War and disease and hunger as a way of life; and they certainly could not have been the forefathers of the Warriors and the Renegades and the twisted minds that nurtured destruction. Surely, he thought as he studied the woman in front of him, the first man must have existed solely to survive, to continue his species, and to grow old in a big round bed surrounded by friends and relatives— and ultimately die happy.

He was drawn back to reality when Crystal leaned back on the couch and her hand fell to her side. "There aren't any answers," she said with absolute certainty, inclining her head toward the window and the ragged lace curtains that hung longer on one side than the other. "And that's the only answer any of us will ever have."

Her eyes were distant as she stared at the gently sloping curve of the land which led up to the barn, and at the swamp rabbit who was eating long blades of grass alongside the path, and whose coal-black eyes were wary and fearful. She sighed gently, folding her arms across her chest until the balloon sleeves of her blouse fell like drapes over her body.

"I can go out there," she continued, inclining her head toward the window, "tell myself that I'm going to find a new path to ride – and it never happens. We always end up right back where we started from – with no more answers than when we first left." She paused, and turned to glance at Raine's questioning eyes once again.

"But somehow," she added with a sudden surge of warmth and love, "I don't think it's the same somewhere else."

92

She leaned forward to rest her elbows on her knees, her hands hanging relaxed just inches from Raine's. "Maybe it's just a simple case of the other man's planet always being greener, but it's a sure bet that it couldn't be any crueler than Terra has become."

Raine's brows narrowed. "You speak as one who had lived through the War might have spoken," he pointed out. "And yet you have obviously lived in a time of relative peace – for the War ended years ago, and rumor has it that the world is recovering." He sounded dubious, even in the telepathic link to my mind. "Some even say the Earth will be a beautiful refuge for those who choose to remain here."

Crystal's eyes closed almost painfully, and for an instant Raine thought he had offended her with some careless choice of words. "I don't *choose* to remain here," she countered, speaking more harshly than she would have intended. She opened her eyes then, and looked at Raine.

He appeared nervous, almost afraid of something even he could not name. Very gently, she reached out and took his hand once again, managing a reassuring smile at his perplexed expression. "But that's enough about me," she decided suddenly. "Let's see what's in the stars for you."

"For me?" Raine repeated, watching her turn his hand over, palm-up. At first, he didn't understand her intent, until suddenly it became clear. "Certainly you don't claim to be able to read the lines of the palm," he said.

She shrugged. "I don't claim anything. But my grandmother used to think I had a talent for deciphering people, so...." She felt him tense, but refused to relinquish his hand as she laughed melodically. "Don't worry," she said, tracing the most prominent line in Raine's hand. "I promise not to hurt you – and that's about the best any of us can hope for, isn't it?" She studied his hand, matched it to her own for a moment, then sighed deeply. "After all, we need all the help we can get just in order to survive — and if some cosmic joker left a roadmap in your palm, what's the harm in trying to figure it out?"

Raine felt himself slowly relaxing, falling into whatever spell this golden star-witch might be casting. He even managed to laugh.

"Life's a game, is that it?" he asked. "And all the people merely gamesters?"

Crystal nodded without looking up. "Something like that," she conceded with a gentle lilt in her voice "Or maybe it's just a War dance, and some of us are too smart to join in."

Her eyes closed then, in the middle of the day which suddenly felt to Raine like some dark and utterly enchanted night. For though he had envisioned Crystal to be a mystical soul, he had not at all imagined that she would display her abilities so openly to someone who was still a stranger. And yet, her straightforwardness captured Raine's imagination almost as much as the more reserved way he had originally pictured her. In his mind, he had created an image of a quiet young woman who thought quiet thoughts and did not choose to speak of them often. But the fact that she had opened to him so quickly left him confused. Was she normally so casual, or was Raine the exception? He settled on the latter image as her eyes reopened.

She took a very deep breath, looked at his palm more closely. "How old are you?" she wondered curiously, almost suspiciously.

"How old do you think I am?" he asked lightly. "How old do the lines in my hand make me to be?"

She studied his handsome features which seemed to shift and change in the sunlight streaming in through the window, studied his palm for another moment, then blinked as if to clear some recurring vision of doom. "Either you're a very old soul in a very young disguise," she ventured bravely, "or else..." Her voice drifted into silence. "Or else," she continued at last, "you've discovered the fountain of youth which old Ponce de Leon was looking for a long time ago. Care to tell me if I'm right or not?" she asked then, her grin becoming more bold and daring. "After all, we mystics need a little validation from time to time just to be sure we're in contact with the right spirits."

Raine stared at her with the expression of a man who had just been struck by lightning, for though her assumption about his age could have been a lucky guess, he did not perceive that to be true. Something told him that he had found whatever answers there were to find – not in Crystal's psychic talent, but in the woman herself. She was everything he had imagined her to be, everything he had hoped she would be... yet she was different, more.

"I... I am..." And his voice faltered into stunned silence as he came up with a weak smile to cover his amazement "Let's just say that I've seen more than my share of sunsets." *And funerals and faces change from soft beauty to old age...*

Raine clamped down on the intruding thought of time, for though Crystal was a young woman now, he wondered if she would be like so many other women he had admired from a distance — faces that changed from innocence to knowledge to passion to resignation to Death. He thought of the whore at the bar – of how she had once been twenty, was now pushing forty, and would, in another moment, be dead. And above all else, Raine did not wish to leave Crystal behind, did not wish to watch her grow old alone and finally wither like some fragile flower in a cold winter wind. He did not wish to remain young forever, and in love with someone who would stay no longer than smoke on an autumn horizon.

"Don't worry," Crystal said quietly, interrupting his morbid train of thought. "I'm not about to roll over and die just yet."

Raine snatched his hand away, only then remembering that physical touch opened all the channels of natural psychic abilities – his and hers combined. She had seen, therefore, his love for her. She had seen his truth and his frustration and his fears and his weaknesses. And yet she continued to smile that wistful half-smile that seemed to be mocking Death itself. He started to stand, to find his way out of the white wood frame house in the middle of a dream, but she grasped him firmly by the wrist, pulling him back down into his chair.

"That's what you came here for, isn't it?" she asked, looking at the eyes which would not return her gaze. "You said you wanted to talk – and what difference does it make if you talk with your mind or your lips?" She took him by the hand once again, ignoring his persistent tug of resistance.

Raine said nothing. He merely stared at the floor, at his feet, at the ragged and frayed bottom of his own pants. Everything was happening too fast, and his mind seemed to have been left somewhere at the base of a thick-barked pine where he had spent the night. "How much did you-?"

But he couldn't say it.

"How much of what you were thinking did I see?" she finished for him presently, her fingertip tracing the lifeline in his palm. She reached out with her other hand to tilt his chin upward, forcing him to meet her eyes. "Enough," she confessed with a sigh that might have been relief, might have been sadness.

But her eyes were bright then, and Raine could not help recognizing his own reflection within them. They were bright with a promise of some intangible thing – some untouchable, unreachable thing that had no name. Some called it love, but love was nothing more than one word in a language on one single planet amidst all the galaxies. It was *more*, the promise in her eyes which mirrored Raine's thoughts. It came in images rather than in words, in thoughts rather than verbal wanderings. It was trees heavy with dew. And it was sunlight on that dew, creating a thousand prismatic rainbows. It was animals warm in their burrows, and children building secret forts in secret places on cold November mornings.

"Enough," she said, breaking the stillness, "to know that I want to see more." But instead of looking at his palm, she studied his face, the ageless beauty which was Raine, the warmth that flowed out from those eyes and seemed to swallow her. Slowly, very slowly, she allowed the moment to solidify around them.

And suddenly, Crystal was as clearly imbedded in my mind as Raine had been for the past century, I could sense her every thought, her every mood, her every image and desire. Her eyes turned dark as she rose from the tattered sofa to walk across the room to the window. During the silences and the conversation and the unceasing march of time, the sun had fallen beneath a distant row of trees, and the scent of azaleas drifted in through the screen to mingle with the warm colors of afternoon.

Raine remained seated, staring at a stain on the carpet and trying to imagine why in all the conceivable worlds he had come here. He had nothing to say, yet everything to say. He had nothing to keep him here, yet nothing seemed endowed with enough power to make him leave. He started to speak, but the words suspended themselves in his throat when she turned from the window and extended her hand.

A small smile came to her lips. "Take my hand." she said quietly, and waited.

At first, Raine made no move to comply. Though he had already touched her, already knew she was irrefutably real, there was something about the act of investing in that reality which frightened him. He shook his head, feeling the fear and the pain well up from some dark place outside of time. "I cannot," he whispered. "For if I... if I allow myself to..." He felt his face darken, hoped she hadn't noticed.

"If you what?" she prompted, kneeling by the chair where he sat. She glanced out the window one last time, watched the final rays of sun as they were consumed by a hungry twilight. Very carefully, she touched his arm, running her fingers down the long-sleeved shirt that fit tight to his skin. "If you touch me, you're afraid you'll want me?"

Raine gave no outward sign that he had heard her at all. His black eyes closed, clouding his mind with pain. "You don't understand," he whispered, at last openly daring to meet her gaze. "You are not... *real*," he stated fervently, grasping the arms of the chair in a desperate attempt to ignore the warm invitation in her eyes. "I have gone mad and created you from my own thoughts. I have envisioned a woman who would say to me the things you have said, a woman who would think thoughts which I could feel in my mind, a woman who would love the... the..." And he fell silent.

But the smile never left her face. "The *quest* for love?" she completed after a moment of silence.

Raine nodded numbly, for the first time learning what it was that he truly wanted – to be forever in *search* of love, to be forever *needing* it, *wanting* it... and maybe to be forever *afraid* to possess it. In that moment, he felt the shame come in around him like a grim blanket of horror. He had loved Aralin, but there was no fire in her eyes. He had loved her, had held her against him, had touched her and made love to her, but she was not the same. She had been straightforward and certain, living in a desert separated from a reality she had had no desire to be a part of. But Crystal....

He would not look up. At that moment, the carpet and the oncoming darkness and the smell of azaleas seemed to be the only other things in existence. Crystal was his own creation, his intimate and private fantasy. And fantasies were often more safe when left in the heart. One could not live a fantasy, Raine reminded himself, trying to ignore the scent of summer which seemed to linger in her hair. And most of all, one could not dare hope for a fantasy to return love.

One could not, therefore, dare to love one's perfect lover.

He struggled for a moment with his own conviction, then took a deep and trembling breath.

"I must go," he stated, forcing detachment on himself and not looking at her as he rose and pulled free of her hand which was still resting on his arm.

He bit back the pain of the severance, tasted the threat of emotions too close to the surface. "I must... never see you again."

98

Crystal laughed out loud, shattering whatever courage Raine had possessed in the instant before.

He looked up, felt his universe shattering, and tried to imagine what she found so amusing.

She stood close to his side, looked into his eyes for a moment, then touched him gently on the shoulder. "Can you do that?" she wondered. "Can you honestly *do* that?"

She paused, removed her hand and let it fall back to her side. "After all," she continued with a tender grin, "if you're like most so-called gods, I don't think you can create something – as you claim to have created me – and then just walk away from it." She shrugged almost indifferently, almost teasingly. "Unless, of course you're claiming to be The One True God."

Her eyes caught the faint afternoon light, and there was more than a hint of amusement in her words when she spoke again. "And if *that's* the case, then you won't have any trouble at all in abandoning your creation." Her eyes scanned the window, the dark outline of the abandoned City silhouetted in the distance. "So go ahead. Walk out that door and never look back." She paused, then gave him the challenge. "But we both know you won't. We both know you *can't*."

Raine did not know what to do. He started to speak, stopped himself, and looked at the door which suddenly seemed a thousand light years away. It was in another reality, and if he chose to walk through it, he knew he could never return. Love was a finicky thing, such a terribly finicky thing indeed. He took one step toward the door, almost expecting, *wanting* her to stop him. But when she didn't, when she simply walked back over to the window and stared out at the darkness, Raine stopped.

"Forgive me," he whispered. "I didn't intend to imply that I literally created you. I simply meant..."

She turned, shook the hair back from her face and pinned him with a look so raw it bled. "Did it ever occur to you that *I* created *you*, too?"

Raine thought for a moment that he would go completely out of his mind. On the one hand, she was such a seemingly indifferent creature, unconcerned with what he did or did not do. But on the other hand, she was as obsessed and fixated on that-which-has-no-name as Raine was himself.

Time stopped. Staggered. Moved forward again. She took a hesitant step toward him.

"If you take my hand, I can show you love," she promised, as if discussing nothing more important than the weather. "It may not be what you expect it to be or what you dreamed it would be, but in this world few things are perfect – and love is perhaps the least perfect thing of all."

She held her hand toward him for a long time, the way one might try to coax a feral kitten, simply waiting for Raine to make whatever decision he was destined to make.

"And what do *you* want?" he asked at last. "For surely you cannot claim to love me." After all, he told himself, he had just walked out of the trees and spoken to her for the first time that morning.

A moment of indecision seemed to cross her features. "Wait here," she instructed, and walked into one of the bedrooms. When she returned a few moments later she was carrying a small book which she handed to Raine – quite hesitantly, he noticed.

"Go ahead," she instructed when he turned questioning eyes in her direction. "Open it"

Raine looked down at the book as one might study a scroll which would foretell one's own future. He caressed the faded maroon cover, running his fingers across the embossed surface.

"What is it?" he wondered, his voice becoming curious and gentle again.

"It's a photo album," she said, and I thought I felt her suppress a shiver of pleasant embarrassment. "Go on," she urged again. "I think you might be surprised."

Raine met her eyes, cautiously at first, but caution and

reservation gradually gave way to trust. He opened the album and gazed down at the first page to find his own unmistakable dark eyes looked back up at him.

"Where did you get these?" he asked, attempting to hide the surprise that went sliding down his spine. There were photos of Raine entering The Round Table, of Raine walking in the forest near our house, of Raine in places which had no name.

Again, she shrugged and took a step closer, looking over his shoulder.

"You really wouldn't believe me if I told you," she warned him with a tender smile. "Let's just say that it doesn't matter now." She took the book from him and laid it aside, then looked up once again, meeting his eyes.

Raine managed a smile, and held out his hand, and, after a brief moment, she accepted.

"I want to know you," he whispered, pulling her close to his chest and abandoning whatever fears remained. He knew he was tempting the Fates, accepting a fantasy that had become a reality, almost daring the dark forces of the universe to try to separate them. "I want..." *To have no wants....*

Very slowly, she put one hand to his lips, silencing him, then reached down to the front of his shirt. She unfastened the buttons slowly, sensually, then slid it from his back in one easy movement. He was lean but powerfully built, and she stole a moment to enjoy the smooth texture of his skin.

Raine trembled beneath her hands, falling ever deeper into azalea-scented madness, powerless to stop it. I could feel his reactions, his love for her, her love for him, and though it was perhaps wrong of me, I could not help falling into both of them myself. They moved together like serpents lethargic from the afternoon sun, twining together, sharing some secret thought that bound them together forever. It became a slow motion dance, an act of conjoining suspended away from time, creator and created (though I was no longer certain which was which) coming together to form one pure and perfect being.

Raine removed the soft blouse she wore with delicate hands, running his fingertips along the artery in her neck, watching her eyes close with pleasure and anticipation. She drew him down onto the floor, pulling him over her, telling him with her eyes and her thoughts that love was not so terribly wrong after all, telling him that there could still be tenderness and passion in a world that had all but forgotten the meaning of those long ago words.

She looked into his eyes as he entered her, as flesh melted away and became trivial, as minds flowed together and thoughts became impossible to distinguish.

Raine was lost unto himself, floating in a void of darkness, and for the first time he could recall, he was at peace. Even with Aralin, there had been a sense of transience, a knowledge that nothing was permanent. But now, lost inside the woman he had molded out of his own dangerous imaginings, the woman who said she had created him in return, he opened himself fully, allowing the love to flow into the woman beneath him, allowing his dreams and his reality to become joined with hers.

She never closed her eyes, Raine noticed, and there was something about that open trust which caused him to realize that all his other loves had been nothing more than fleeting illusions. Lovers who closed their eyes were hiding, he thought as he gave himself to her and took her for himself. Lovers who closed their eyes were the most fearful and therefore the most damned of all the pitiful creatures on Earth.

He ran his hands across her body, let his thoughts travel gently through her mind, and tried not to imagine what it would be like the next time they made love, or if indeed there would ever be a next time.

*

Raine stayed with Crystal for three years – until the time

he left Terra in search of answers, until he came to realize that love alone could not sustain him indefinitely, despite his deepest desire for that to be a higher truth. During those three years, however, I have no doubt that Raine was finally happy. He spent his days tending the gardens around our home, conversing quietly with me and with the land, and he spent his evenings with Crystal, talking of wild creatures, lying under the black canopy of night while the stars made their eternal walk across the sky, making love. Occasionally, he would bring Crystal to our home, and there the three of us would share a quiet dinner, after which we would slip into the bedroom and sleep soundly in a bed that seemed to enjoy the addition of feminine warmth.

Crystal was one of those creatures for which there is no logical explanation. For though she would be compelled to love Raine forever, she would often express her feelings to me as well — telling me in words or images or in simple gestures that I was part of what she shared with her beloved, that I could possess her and hold her or even make love to her if I had chosen to do so. And, oh, that I could bring those times back!

I was too moralistic or as Raine once jokingly said, too *frightened*, for I never did more with Crystal than deep friendship would allow. We laughed at nothing in particular; we cried over the litter of pups Raine found abandoned and half-starved under the porch one morning; we slept together; and we held one another tightly when the weather turned toward winter. (And Crystal, would that we could have shared more.)

For a time, it was a safe and relatively easy life for the three of us, yet there came the day early in spring when Raine decided that he had spent enough time in Central Florida, and approached us about the possibility of relocating to another part of the country. He had always held a particular fascination for the oceans – for the rocks and the faces carved in them, and for the Pacific coastline which they guarded like sentient stone sentinels.

For myself, and I suspect for Crystal, I would have been content to remain forever in a land that had been kind to us, to stay with the small green garden and the tiny wood frame house that had seen better times, and the sound of mockingbirds singing lonely songs to a silver sky at dawn. But Raine was in our blood, and to make him happy, we both agreed to the move without so much as a major discussion. Raine informed us that he had already checked into the logistics of the matter, and that Relocation Central would permit us to move to a small flat in San Diego in exchange for three other people who would come to inhabit our home.

Perhaps that is when Raine first thought of leaving Terra altogether, and perhaps Crystal or myself should have tried to dissuade him from his decision to succumb to the wanderlust in his heart. For once we had packed the few things we would need for the trip and had arranged passage on a commercial airline, I believe something changed deep inside Raine which eventually led to his departure on the *Dorsai*.

I only know that things began to change once we reached San Diego. The air there was somehow different, and though the land had rebuilt itself following the War, there were still signs to remind us that Terra was no longer the beautiful woman she had been in her youth.

The apartment we had taken was nicer than the house we had shared in Central Florida, and the money Crystal had gotten from selling the ranch helped in making the place into a livable and even comfortable home.

Yet there was a sterility and a loneliness that accompanied living in sight of any large body of water. We were located hanging precariously on the edge of a hillside in what had once been a fashionable neighborhood, but which had deteriorated following the War. Now, a century after the last bombs had fallen, flowers had started to creep up the sides of the hill, and the canyon below the apartment was filled with the sounds of coyotes in the evening and seabirds during the afternoon.

By standing on the balcony outside the bedroom, one could see the Pacific Ocean stretched out like some lazy whale sleeping on the horizon, its steamy breath transforming to fog in the early morning. There was a sense of peace here, a sense of permanence, but also a deep and abiding sense of melancholy. For as well as being able to see the natural beauty of the ocean, we could also see the now-antique planes which had fallen like injured birds onto the coarse beige sands. We wondered among ourselves from time to time as to why no one had had the decency to remove the wreckage — and were told by small Mexican children with tanned round faces that the City Fathers had decided to leave the planes as a reminder to future generations that War was not quite so easily swept under a cheap shag rug.

For nearly two months, we spent the days exploring the canyon which led down to the shore, and the evenings wrapped warmly in front of the fireplace that was pleased to devour pieces of scrap wood gathered in the wilderness. In the evening, it was not uncommon to see rockets lifting off from Vandenberg, trailing soot and smoke and flame, and lighting the silhouette of those fallen leviathans who would forever look out to the lonely, dark sea.

It was in those evenings that Raine would become restless, and would begin to pace solemnly back in forth in front of the large sliding glass door that overlooked the canyon. Sometimes he would stay up until morning, and once he informed me that he had seen what appeared to be a campfire in the canyon. He said he could not help but wonder if some unfortunate soul was attempting to live off the wild rabbits and ducks who made their home in the urban wilderness. More likely, he decided, the fire was simply started by some errant child and a book of matches.

It was safer to think that. Less painful.

*

On the night it changed forever, Crystal was lying in the macramé hammock on the balcony off the bedroom. Raine was sitting quietly on the wooden beams of the balcony, as if tempting the Fates to produce an earthquake to send him sprawling over the edge and down into the rocky gorge below. The night was still and utterly black, and as I sat on the faded tweed sofa in the living room, I could hear the muted strains of their conversation. For awhile, it was nothing more than a comforting drone which I attempted to ignore, not wanting to intrude on the privacy of warm nothings whispered solely for the benefit of the cool, bright evening.

But as the night grew later and the sounds of conversation became stronger, I could not help but feel the emotions stirring to life out there on the wooden balcony that creaked and groaned occasionally.

There had been rumors for quite some time concerning the possibility of a mass relocation and colonizing of the twin moons of Altair, and though Raine had never shown any particular interest in being a pioneer, I could feel his thoughts surging toward space as he sat there just staring at the golden eyes of the evening. For a moment, I wanted to climb noisily into his mind, tell him without speaking that men such as himself were not destined to settle down on any world – Terran *or* alien – and work nine to five for the sole purpose of putting food on an Early American dining table each evening at 7 o'clock. Yet even if I had had the courage to take that step into Raine's mind, I do not believe he would have heeded my warning. Perhaps he was basking in Crystal's thoughts, picking up stray images from her mind of what it might be like to travel among the stars as freely as man had once traveled along the now deserted California freeways.

And perhaps that is the moment Raine consigned himself to his Fate.

His eyes were affixed to some distant point of light in the night sky, and he sighed deeply. "Tell me, Crystal," he

106

murmured with a gentle smile, "do you believe there is a remarkable difference between love here on Terra and love elsewhere?"

A faint smile come to Crystal's lips as she cast a glance at him out the corner of deep green eyes. "Perhaps love does not exist anywhere else, Raine," she suggested, her own eyes fixed to some totally different point of light in the cosmos. "Perhaps we poor crazy humans are the only creatures of the universe who seem to draw nourishment from the mental energy we have named 'love'."

She fell silent for a moment, drew her legs underneath herself, then sat up to look out over the black ocean. On the horizon, a ship's lights were flickering through the haze, and a foghorn sounded far in the gray distance.

"Perhaps Terrans alone are doomed to feel loneliness and regret and joy and all the other emotions that govern our lives from the day we're born into this world." She shrugged, and did not look at Raine, for perhaps she was already beginning to sense the permeating restlessness within him. Or maybe she was simply experiencing the same sense of being lost that the captain of that ship on the horizon must certainly have felt. She watched the dim white lights for a second longer, until they slipped from sight as if the entire ship had been swallowed whole by some angry serpent god of the sea. Then, with a sigh, she closed her eyes.

For a moment, Raine merely pondered her words, but gradually his own curious nature asserted itself. "I've heard rumors of the worlds out there," he said almost to himself, "and legend tells us that Terrans are incapable of feeling true, unselfish love. Legend has it that the Centaurians and the Altairians and all the other creatures who inhabit this void are far more mature in the ways of love than we Terrans shall ever hope to be."

Crystal laughed gently, then slipped from the hammock onto the floor of the balcony to sit close to Raine's side. "Tell me of it then," she entreated, stroking his leg affectionately with one hand. "What have you heard – and from whom?"

Raine looked down at her for a moment, then slowly pushed the long blonde hair back from her face. But his eyes returned to the stars. "A transport captain once told me that love on Alicron VI is a somewhat peculiar matter indeed," he reported, mentally searching for Alicron somewhere among all the other stars. "He said that the Alicronians spend the majority of their lives in seclusion — and that, once every twenty years, when they feel the molecules of the universe have given them enough energy, they come down from their mountaintops and give that love away."

He shook his head with a weary sound. "He said that the Alicronians define love as warmth, security and mystery – most of all, mystery." Again, came the absent-minded laughter which was filled with bitterness, irony, and perhaps even envy. "Terrans, on the other hand, seek to gain love from others – to *take* warmth, security, and solve all the mysteries rather than simply appreciating them."

Crystal leaned closer against Raine's legs and rested her head against his thigh. "But is it worth the twenty years in seclusion?" she wondered. "Is *anything* worth loneliness – even love?"

Raine looked at her for a long time. "Perhaps we shall never know." Then, with a graceful movement, he got to his feet, reached down, and gently pulled Crystal up to stand by his side. "Come with me." he asked gently, inclining his head toward the shoreline. "I need to be..."

But he shook his head, feeling one of those emotions for which there was no name yet assigned.

In my own mind, I felt it too, and though it is probably futile to attempt to explain the mysteries, I believe his feelings were vaguely related to a deep form of grief. And though he never would have believed it on a conscious level, it is possible he was resentful that the one woman whom he loved more than life itself could never seek to unravel the mysteries of the universe with him. The most he could hope for on Terra would be long walks down a black shoreline in the night. The most Terra could give him was a muted view of the stars and a longing to know more, and the distinct, ever-present knowledge that he could not keep his beloved and sail the galactic seas, too.

Despite the fact that Raine and Crystal both asked for my company, I did not go with them when they left the house that evening. But throughout the long night, images continued to come. Images of Raine's thoughts — dark and filled with love for Crystal and the stars, yet suddenly it was not clear which was the top priority. I knew they would make love out there in the shadow of one of those fallen metal birds, and with a soul-deep despair, I knew it would be the last time.

*

For a very long time, they walked, going nowhere in particular, yet journeying to every conceivable star in the multiverse. Crystal spoke of Altair and Regulus as if she had traveled there hundreds of times in rockets and starships constructed solely in her own thoughts. She told Raine of a stream on Cephalon IX which had a pale blue glow on dark nights when the triple moons were new in a virgin sky and Cephalon VIII hung low on the horizon. And Raine told her of Terra before the War – when exotic flowers with long and complicated names grew in secluded valleys and on unmarred hillsides, oblivious to the bombs that would one day destroy them. He told her of his past lovers (which he had never done before), of Aralin and Desiree and Miguel and Anthony – and how each one had had some particular scent, some different smile, some faintly different embrace and individual touch.

"And each of them is gone now," he whispered, looking out to sea and listening to the muted and distant cry of an invisible night bird that was only a foghorn. "Each of them has vanished from Earth just as quietly and as anonymously as those flowers on grassy hillsides, beloved," Raine said, not looking at Crystal just then.

I knew then that it wasn't love and hate who were mirror twins. The final irony was that *grief* would always turn out to be the paradoxical antithesis and simultaneous manifestation of whatever it is that humans call love.

She remained silent and walked a few steps away from Raine – further down the shoreline, until she stood under the wing of one fallen Phantom. She thought of the ship she had seen from the balcony of our home, and though it had long since disappeared over the dark and treacherous abyss of the ocean, its image lingered clearly in her thoughts. On that ship was a man, she thought. A terribly lonely man who made no great difference to the flow of time or the memory of the galaxy. A man who, like Raine, was compelled to keep moving and look only ahead and never behind. A man who could not afford the luxury of waving goodbye to friends on shore.

At last, she turned toward her beloved and watched him watching the darkness. He stood only a few feet away, yet the images in my mind said he might as well have been a million light years off in the void. He was lost to her in that instant out-of-time, just as lost and impossible to find as the light from that ship which had vanished over the horizon.

And yet, with the courage – or possibly the desperation – of a lover, she moved toward the darkened silhouette on the shoreline and placed one hand on his shoulder.

"Who are you?" she wondered quietly, following his gaze out to sea. "Right now, in this moment alone, Raine, *who are you*?"

Raine did not turn from where his eyes were locked to some particular swell in the sea, and for one of the first times, he truly understood that he did not know. He covered her hand with his own, leaning his cheek down against their joined fingers.

"Who do you want me to be?" he asked, attempting to

hide his own sense of displacement as a green ball of light fell from the sky and seemed to drop out of sight into the ocean. "Falling stars, my love. Make a wish on them and tell me who you want me to be."

But he did not wait for her to respond, undoubtedly afraid that the wish she made would not be one he could honor. "Perhaps I am some lost soul of the past who had developed a most peculiar immunity to Death. Or perhaps, my treasured Crystal..." His voice trailed into silence, joining with the stillness of the night and the haunted murmur of the ocean. "Or perhaps, I am no one at all... and will never be anything more than the sum of that."

Crystal moved closer behind him, pressing the warmth of her body against him. I do not know what she was feeling, or if indeed she was experiencing any emotion at all. It is entirely possible that Raine's displacement had edged its way into her mind and severed her from reality — just as he had done to me decades ago. I know only that she loved him — and that her love, like the ocean and the blackness and the stars, was the only certainty at that time.

"Would that make you different than everyone else?" she inquired quietly. "Would it make you any better or any worse than the rocket builders or the people who work at Luna City?" She fixed her eyes on some star that was barely visible to the naked eye, secretly hoping Raine was looking at that same dim point of light. "No man or woman can be more than they are, Raine. All we can be is what the Fates have decreed, and all we can hope for is a gentle transformation to whatever might happen next."

After a long moment of deliberation, Raine turned slowly to face her, to look into the mystical green eyes that had enslaved him years ago. For a brief instant, she was a stranger to him – just as he was becoming a stranger to himself. It was one of those moments when one person truly looks at another and realizes in a flash of horror that each individual is lost and utterly alone inside himself.

111

He gazed on Crystal and did not know who she was. She was beautiful, she was familiar, she had blonde hair and dark green eyes and she was wearing one of those smiles that had been able to send his melancholy away in the past. And yet, she was nothing more than the combination of her features, the sum of her physical form, the totality of one single person who was only slightly more familiar than a stranger.

Raine felt himself start to panic, and watched the mental transformation with remarkable detachment. He, too, was someone else, and the *real* Crystal and Raine were sitting in a theatre watching these two fictional characters on a screen as tall as the sky, but a screen that depicted only black and white in a two-dimensional void. He could almost smell the mildew and musk and all the other scents indigenous to theatres. Worst of all, he could feel the masks worn by the actors, the claustrophobia of those masks tightening around his face as the mask became the unwanted new identity.

He tried to speak, to change the course and direction of the play unfolding in front of him, but something held him still and mute, making him small and insignificant in comparison to the image on the screen. He tasted the sad bitterness of someone who had seen a very sad film for the fifth time – watching, experiencing emotions that were not entirely their own – knowing that the outcome would always be the same. One could not change something that had been preordained in the molecules of the universe herself. Rhett Butler would always walk out on Scarlet O'Hara and Old Yeller would always die, and the real Raine and Crystal would be forever destined to part.

He shoved the intruding thought away, but not before recognizing its painful truth. The film had already been made, and the actors had no choice but to speak their lines and make their exits. There were no alternate endings on the cutting room floor.

Then, in a last desperate attempt to alter the reality of true reality, he put his arms around the strange woman on the

112

shore and drew her against him as if to block the suddenly empty spot located precisely in the middle of his chest.

"If I am never to be anything more in the future," he whispered, managing a weak and unfelt smile solely for her benefit, "then I am pleased that I have been something in the past, even if that something was recognized only by one other person."

Crystal shook her head sadly, then leaned her cheek against Raine's chest, inhaling the intoxicatingly spicy fragrance that was so much a part of him. "*Two* other people," she corrected, committing the scent and the beauty and the aloofness of him to memory forever. "For surely Fogg is as much a part of your life as anyone can ever be."

Raine started to speak, to protest the sudden hopelessness in her voice, but she silenced him with one finger placed gently against his lips. "He'll be with you forever," she pointed out with a sense of comfort. "Fogg will be by your side until the last rocket leaves Terra – and *then* some. You really can't ask for much more than that, Raine – to have someone to share it all with."

Raine felt tears in the corners of his eyes, but blinked them back and chose a point above Crystal's head to fix his gaze. "Fogg is a beloved friend," he stated, tasting the flavor of friendship on his tongue as he spoke the word "But you... " He chanced a brief glance at her, only to see her looking far off into the distance, out to sea, out toward the future, away from Terra and home. "But *you*... you are what I have been seeking since my first memories began! You are what I was searching for in Aralin and Miguel and all the others." He shook his head, feeling the black cloak of panic close over him, threatening to drown him in an ocean far more vast than the one by which he was standing. "You are more than *life* to me!"

But Crystal only shook her head with a certain amount of finality. "You said it yourself, Raine, long ago, on that day we first met at the barn." She stroked his hair, savoring the feel of him, the warmth of him... knowing it was already beginning to fade. "You said then that you're in love with the *quest* for love, and there's nothing so terribly wrong with that."

Her eyes traveled upward, toward the stars and the black blood of space. "It's just that I can't go with you." There was no bitterness in her statement. Instead, her thoughts were permeated with the colors of futility and irony... and utter certainty. Again, she stroked his hair, brushing it back from his eyes, feeling the smooth warmth of his face.

"You forget that I can read your mind sometimes, Raine," she reminded him. "And sometimes I forget that you can read mine." After a moment, she released him, then stepped away as one might step away from an animal that was being sent back to the wild. There might have been tears in her eyes, but most likely she had resigned herself to this some time in the past. "I know what you're thinking — and I want you to go." She inclined her head upward, but would not look at the stars They were her rivals now.

"When I was a kid," she continued, not immediately noticing Raine's stunned and utterly pained expression, "my grandmother used to take me out on the porch at night and tell me bedtime stories." She shrugged, attempting to portray an air of indifference toward Raine which she would never truly feel. She began to pace back and forth at the edge of the shoreline, stopping at the wing of the downed plane, then back again. "She always sat in this old wooden rocking chair that creaked." She laughed in fond reminiscence, but even I could hear the bitterness in it now — the bitterness that lived in the memories of a lonely child. I heard it, Raine heard it, and there was nothing either of us could do to ease the pain or send the hurt away. I felt a tear fall onto a cheek which was not my own.

"Anyway," she continued, her voice sounding very small and uncertain. "One night, she was sitting there in her rocker and we were watching one of the rockets leaving from Canaveral. That was in the old days, when they were still building Luna City and more than half of those rockets never made it into orbit."

Raine moved toward her, but she motioned him away.

"No," she said. "I want you to hear this." She looked at him then, met his eyes, shared his torment. And she smiled very tenderly as she sat down on the shoreline and cold sea water licked against her legs. "I want to tell you the story my grandmother told me, Raine." She just sat there for a long time, shivering against the cold she couldn't even feel. I felt it for her, and so did Raine. "Maybe someday... maybe *someday*, Raine, you can tell it to your own grandchildren."

A sad little wind blew across the face of the ocean, ventured onto the land, and beckoned Raine to sit by her side.

"It was in the middle of summer," Crystal began, "and the horses were standing in the front pasture. It was dreadfully hot that night, hot and muggy, and the wind was still as the eyes of a dead man. The stallion, Kingsley, was half asleep, but Antoinette and her foal were looking at that rocket, too. I could see the foal's eyes, and they were wide as the summer sky, all full of wonder and curiosity at the strange flaming bird which was just passing over the house. The foal started to run, just running wild around and around the pasture like he was trying to follow that rocket until it was out of sight. He pawed at the ground when it was gone, and I could hear him snorting and calling for it to come back and take him with it – to take him away from Terra." She shook her head and sighed very deeply.

"That's when my grandmother told me about the stars for the first time." She paused and brushed the hair back from her face and listened to the secrets in the wind for just a moment. "She said that there's a star for everyone, and that each star represents one person who has lived on Terra. Every star has a name, and when a new baby is born, the gods give the name of that baby to a star. That's a common old legend, I guess..."

She paused and time went by. Slowly. Not slowly enough.

"But what made it so real was that Grandma was stroking my hair, Raine... and I'll never forget that night. She was

115

stroking my hair and there was a crack in her voice whenever she spoke. She showed me my mother's star, and said she still remembered the night that star had been named. She said my mother had been a breach birth, and that even the gods were afraid they wouldn't get to name a new star that night."

Crystal stopped for a moment, and looked far out to sea again, but never up to the sky, never at the stars. I don't think she would ever want to see those night-bright eyes again. They were too close: too close to the past, to childhood, to more simple times when every question was somehow answered.

"But when I asked my grandmother to show me her star, she pulled me a little closer to her side and said that no one was allowed to know which star was their own."

She shrugged, seemingly indifferent to the whole melancholy matter. "She said that she could show me my mother's star or my father's star, or the star of all the king's men... but she couldn't show me which was hers... or even tell me which was mine." She reached out and picked up a piece of broken shell lying close to her side. She tossed it out to sea, into the darkness, into the night. "Grandma said that if you ever knew – *really knew* – which star was your own, you'd always be reaching for it, and you'd always be unhappy because you couldn't quite get there from here. She said that once a person found out which star had their name on it, they couldn't sleep at night or fall in love or do anything other than wonder what was on all the worlds circling that one little light in the sky." She looked pointedly at Raine. "She even said that sometimes the gods wouldn't let you die if you found out which star belonged to you."

She looked away from Raine, but the loneliness in her voice and the sadness which drifted across the canyon and came to where I was sitting in the living room of our apartment was a tangible, living death. It was the death of love, which was, ironically, both its resurrection and its benediction.

116

"The last thing my grandmother said that night was that maybe, one day, I would be able to find her star for her. She believed that I'd make it, Raine," Crystal said very quietly. "She thought I'd go out there and find the star with her name on it, then come home to Terra to tell her all the things that were there." She laughed, but in my own mind, it felt much more like a sob. She looked at Raine once again, forcing him to meet her eyes.

"But I can't do it, my friend," she told him finally. "I can't go out there anymore than that old woman in the wooden rocker could have gone."

Raine reached for her, but she shook her head and managed a ragged smile. "Don't you see, Raine?" she asked "Don't you *know*?"

Raine did not speak, and whether it was from fear of shattering the moment or his inability to command words, I do not know. He merely looked at her, like a photographer envisioning the perfect angle in his mind; and then he looked away, capturing the picture for all eternity in his memory alone.

"No," he whispered at last, shivering against the water that was lapping more persistently against his legs. "No, Crystal... I do not."

She touched him on the cheek, tilting his head upward, forcing him to confront the night sky which now seemed to own him.

"You've seen your own star, my love," she told him. "And now you can do nothing but try to reach it." She smiled again, very softly, as if to tell him that it shouldn't hurt so very much. "It doesn't matter whether you call that star Regulus or Omicron or Ceti, or Willow or Raine. What matters is that you've seen it, and you've chosen to call it Love."

Raine shook his head as if in denial of the simple truth she had spoken, but in his mind I could see that there was no way he could reverse his destiny. He reached for her once again, and was almost surprised when she made no effort to retreat.

In his heart, I felt the heaviness, the loss, the bitterness and, most of all, the grief. And yet, intermixed with all the melancholy emotions, he knew a sense of elation, a new sense of freedom for which he would eternally damn himself. But he pulled her to him – desperately – and made one final attempt to dissuade reality from its course.

"I cannot leave you behind," he whispered close to her ear, closing his eyes to blot away the image of the stars which seemed to be taking him away. "I *cannot*..."

But she placed one finger against his lips as he lay back in defeat on the cold, wet sand. He opened his eyes, and she caught him looking at the stars of all the souls who had ever trekked the face of Terra... and in his gaze she could see the stars' reflection.

"You already have, my love," she said.

She closed her own eyes, rested her head on his chest, and found herself wishing for blindness and darkness and death... for both of them.

*

We remained in the apartment for another three months — carrying on with the pretense that nothing had changed, and that nothing ever would. But I suspect Raine was merely attempting to bargain with the Fates or bribe the gods or alter his own nature during that time. Things *had* changed, from the moment they left the apartment that evening, there was no turning back, no going home, no altering the script. We knew it even if we did not openly acknowledge it.

Raine changed from being quiet and philosophical to being boisterous and outgoing – from being lonely and sad to being drunk and utterly blissful in the company of friends whom he invited over on a nightly basis. It was as if he were attempting to change his soul into one that would not match the name on the star that had been assigned to him by the gods themselves.

His success was minimal... and on the Fifth day of F'alyn he walked solemnly into the dilapidated travel office on the Avenue and booked passage on the *Dorsai*.

I do not know what goodbyes he said to Terra, and I am certain that he said none to Crystal. But before leaving San Diego, he went to the local animal shelter, purchased a faded orange tomcat who was slated for an early morning euthanasia, and left him purring peacefully on the foot of the bed where Crystal was sleeping. Then, with eyes that gleamed with madness and a certain amount of horror, he took me to the bus terminal and we boarded the leviathan bound for Nevada.

Perhaps the Fates and the gods and his own nature will forgive Raine someday.

And someday, perhaps Crystal will, too.

END TRANSMISSION Fogg
Communications #413877989.K

———————

Beloved Crystal:

I hope Fogg is right – that you will one day be able to forgive me for what I have done to the only thing we ever really had. I see now that space is indeed endless, as poets have surmised throughout the centuries, and the sad thing is that there is only more "nothing" on the other side of any reality. Legend has it that the end of the universe is actually situated just outside the edge of darkness that extends beyond where telescopes can see. However, I cannot help but think that, as we move further and further into this void, new telescopes will be devised that can see beyond that alleged "end".

One day we are going to be amazed to discover that infinity is actually something more than just a horrifying and incomprehensible concept. Why is it, beloved, that Man must seek to confine himself to that which he can understand? Why must we convince ourselves that the end of it all will be found one bright and sunny summer afternoon? Is it because we cannot conceive of the existence of something that knows no bounds? Is it that the universe, like love, must somehow be defined, in the finite mind of Man?

After leaving Trellius, we spent a period of time merely wandering about the populated areas of the galaxy, attempting to earn enough credits to exchange for the Cold Sleep and the journey on toward the Outerworlds where we will be bound by the time you receive this transmission.

For a time, I believe both Fogg and myself touched that mystical illusion known to Terrans as happiness – or, at the very least, we discovered some vague form of contentment. There is a mountain on Ceti Trianguli, which is said to possess magical properties, and for awhile both Fogg and I were content to sit on that mountaintop like the ancient monks of Tibet and simply stare out at the crowded galaxy at night. From that mountain, beloved, one can see all the stars in the galaxy, or so legend has it. In reality, we could observe alien and Terran rockets coming and going with their tails of white flame chasing them all the while. Great starships hung suspended above this small world, and lighted industrial platforms floated on their antigravs like hawks or eagles soaring above the mountains. It was amusing to sit there in our makeshift tent, trying to imagine what souls were inhabiting those anonymous points of light. It seemed to us that the mountain itself was altogether deserted, and were it not for our own pressing need to feed our insanity by moving on out into the galaxy, it is entirely possible that we might have remained there forever.

Trees with broad gold leaves and pale green trunks grew from the top of the mountain, and in the evening when the moons were full and light shone down from the platforms, those leaves would fall to the ground, sparkling like golden tears of the gods in the pale and glittering light. Occasionally, children would came near our campsite in the daytime, gathering the leaves in tattered sacks, then racing away, leaving only their laughter in the wind. Then, early in the evening, there would be great fires some distance away, down the sides of the mountain. The musky scent of smoke would drift up to our campsite, and brilliant blue sparks could be seen rising into the air. The chemicals in the leaves caused the fire to sing and whistle and, some said, to speak in alien tongues.

Once we heard music — sad and lonely and unmistakably Terran in origin. A woman was singing to Earth and Sol — and it made me wonder why she had left her home to begin with. There was melancholy and homesickness in her voice as she sang of autumn and darkness and times before the War. Fogg began to cry, and only then did I understand how terribly selfish I have been.

Unfortunately, he would not allow me to convince him to return to Terra. Probably because he knows that a home, once abandoned, cannot help but change.

And Fogg, like us, beloved, cannot bear to look back on the past and contemplate things which have been but are no longer.

Alas, my friend, I must close now. It is late, and the fires are whispering once again. Tomorrow, we leave this enchanted place and journey outward.

And, oh that we were coming home....

Always,
Raine
Communications #8190008DEC

PS – I shall wait to hear from you before sending the remainder of Fogg's novel – which he says he will be completing soon. He tells me that the story of us is over (at least on paper, though I cannot destroy this hope within me that tells me we shall one day be reunited in reality), and that the remainder of his words will deal with whatever answers there are for Man to find out here in the darkness. I hope the answers (if indeed there are any) will be pleasant, and that they will uncover a way to reunite us before jack o'lanterns burn brightly on Terra.

Tell me of your life on the farm, and if you can find me with your thoughts, send a warm embrace in the still of the evening. At the very least, beloved, think of me when you can.

PPS – Is it Spring on Terra yet? One loses track of time out here....

Dearest Raine:

I have debated over whether I should send this transmission at all. For you see, my beloved, I know now that I shall never see you again. Even if you should decide to return to Terra, I do not think we could ever rebuild what we once held so important. As you stated, time changes people, and sometimes people attempt to change time.

It is unfortunate, but the latter is simply not within the realm of possibility – at least not for me.

You and Fogg have been quite successful in holding Time still and captive, yet we mortals who are still privileged (?) to inhabit old Terra have not been so lucky. I have spoken with a friend of Collette's who is a physicist at Lunaport, and he has informed me that your time and mine are now of two totally different and unconnected realities. I do not pretend to comprehend all the intricacies, but I can grasp enough of what he said to know that, even if you began a return voyage to Terra tomorrow, I would be an old woman by the time you reached the blue horizon of Earth. Forgive me, but I could not bear to have you see me as I am becoming – as I will <u>be</u> by the time this transmission reaches you.

Yes, it is spring on Terra, and has been spring eleven times since your departure from this life. Again, forgive me. I realize you are not dead, but I must force myself to think of you as if you were, for I know that the only time we shall be reunited is if the myths of an afterlife are true. While I am not old by your standards – or even by the standards that existed before the War – my thirty-four years have not treated me kindly. Ah, Raine, is it true that in the days before the War, this was the age considered to be the very prime of ones life? Perhaps I am merely embittered over the fact that none of us on Terra shall live to see sixty, or perhaps I am lamenting the fact that the Earth will have the audacity to continue on without me once I am gone.

Either way, it makes little difference now. The paradoxes of time and space which the physicist attempted to explain to me have sealed our separation. In the beginning, during the first "year" (my Terran year which was probably no more than a moment to you in the arms of hyperspace), I did not fully understand that we are no longer part of the same world. What seems like a year to you is ten for me, ten for Terra... and only a second in your immortal forever.

I had not intended to be maudlin. In fact, I am doing quite well now that I have resigned myself to this reality. As I mentioned, I have returned to the ranch where I grew up – and other than the spring crop of foals and a few additional shingles fallen from the house, not much has changed.

The Renegades have been all but stopped by the new Suburban Peacekeeping Force, and all is quiet in the evenings. The City has rebuilt itself into the metropolis it once was, even though the light pollution has sorely altered my view of the stars. But those few who noticed have been assured that it is necessary – that the rocket builders and the technicians and the enterprising souls who make a pretense of running this world must work around the clock to construct enough rockets to handle the demand for off-world relocation of families and corporations.

I keep imagining I shall awaken one overcast morning to discover that everyone has left Terra once and for all and that I am quite alone. I do not believe this would frighten me, and perhaps it would be a well-deserved twist of fate. My grandmother once told me that happiness is a taxable luxury – and that anyone who becomes too happy (yes, even for the short amount of time we shared, beloved) must eventually repay the gods for those forbidden moments.

I hope this will not change your opinion of me, but I have taken in a couple of roommates. One is named Hendrich, the other is Claret, and both have managed to provide considerable help around the ranch. Hendrich is a young man who reminds me of Fogg – reserved and quiet and apparently an empath to some degree. He is fair-haired and fair-eyed, and doesn't seem to need awkward verbal commands when training the horses. He simply tells them with his mind and they listen. Too bad he can't command politicians and rocket builders and viruses as well! Claret, his friend, is a few years younger than myself, and is one of those women who seems to be endowed with certain mystical powers since her birth in the ruins of Ceylon. She has foretold the futures of presidents and corporate heads and men and women who drink too much, yet she will tell me nothing of my own future. Whenever I have asked her, she only smiles and says that one day perhaps I will find the thing I have lost. Yet I wonder if she knows how very far lost that thing is...

But no matter. I have given them room and food for over two years now, and have developed a fondness for the two of them that makes the night a trifle warmer and allows the days to pass more quickly. Claret is now pregnant with Hendrich's child, and I am considering bearing a child of his myself. Claret tells me that I am not too old to bear children, and that if anything should "happen" to me, she would care for the child as her own. I think they will stay with me here on the ranch and on Terra until...? At this point, I have made no definite decision regarding the possibility of motherhood, but am I just being sentimental in my desire to leave something tangible behind for Terra?

Please, beloved, forgive me for this final transmission. I do not want to sadden you or throw darkness on your star-lighted path. Yet I felt I must share the truth with you – the truth being that Time has had her way with us. If you wish to continue communicating with me, I will welcome and treasure your letters. If not, I cannot blame you, and I shall always love you.

I will send warm thoughts and an embrace in the cool evenings, and hope that time and distant and divergent realities will permit them to reach you. And if it is any consolation to either of us, I will be waiting for you in whatever reality there may be after this Earth is finished with me.

Always... or until [whichever comes {inst)
Crystal
Communication #DD99.Orlando.bimodal

PS – Please send Fogg's novel via transmission as soon as possible. I want to know what finally becomes of the two of you. And, am I being selfish once again, to hope that perhaps you_will be waiting for me in some reality beyond this one?

———————

It was morning on Lazali — a pale, iridescent time of day when the twin white moons were setting beneath a dusky horizon and children could be heard complaining of the long and tedious walk to school in the oncoming desert heat. We had taken a small flat on the south side of Semillon City, and I awoke to watch the seemingly universal cockroach crawling down the wall above our heads, its long antennae searching the still air for some scent of food. It was oddly comforting to know that a small piece of Terran fauna had found its way across an entire galaxy and was now scavenging for dropped morsels and filth in a tenement on Lazali.

Raine was sleeping next to me, black hair falling across dark eyes, lips parted in a smile for the woman who was asleep and dreaming of him back on Terra. He stirred gently as I tapped the wall to send the roach skittering away, and finally opened his eyes. Those same eyes that had so fascinated me in a grove in Florida were now almost terrifying. We both seemed to know instinctively that Lazali would hold the key to our answers, and perhaps Raine had come to fear those answers as much as he craved the knowledge contained within them

When the transport first landed here and we were awakened from the Cold Sleep, Raine looked at me with that same expression of knowledge and said simply, "It is here, Fogg. It is certainly *here*."

Perhaps it was nothing more than the hollow hope that settled in our veins anytime a Transport landed on a new world — the hope that constrained us to believe with all our hearts and minds that the answers were indeed at the tips of our fingers. Our search had, in all, taken over a year now by Terran time calculation, and only the gods know how long we had wasted in "real" space time, and though four months of that "year" had been spent in the icy womb of the Sleepmother on the transport, we were weary and tired and secretly disheartened. We had learned from the transport's captain that jobs for outworlders were scarce on Lazali, and he

jokingly promised to pick us up again in ninety years or so –
when we had had ample time to earn return passage to Terra.

But the Lazalites themselves were a most strange and
beautiful people. Physically, they could have been Raine's
forefathers, for the women were strongly built and dark, and
the men were ebony-eyed enigmas who spoke little, thought
much, and seemed to understand Raine and his quest from
the moment he first stumbled wearily into the tenement and
produced the last of our earnings to secure a room. The young
boy who operated the hotel simply smiled at him, then at me,
and told Raine that boarding and food were free to those who
sought ethereal answers. In short, we were given lodging and
necessities for apparently nothing other than our lofty goals.

That alone should have been a dire warning.

We stayed at the hotel nearly two weeks, walking the
deserts by day and combing the bars by night, until the
morning when the children were complaining more loudly
than usual and the roach was crawling closer to our heads,
and Raine was looking at me with those expressive eyes that
were showing real fear for the first time I could recall. On that
day, he rose without speaking or even an image of warmth in
his mind, and tugged worn clothing onto his body as I
absently followed suit. There seemed little else to do, and I
knew our search was about to end.

As soon as we were dressed, he walked out the front door
of the tenement without breakfast, and continued through the
clay streets and alleys for hours. I do not know precisely what
he was looking for, and I am not at all certain that he knew
himself. He was merely searching for *something* as some men
have sought grails and swords and blue roses. We had
trudged these same nameless streets every day since our
arrival on Lazali, and we had taken no jobs, for Raine
maintained that we would not be staying very long. He knew
that his answer had to be *here* or else it did not exist in all the
galaxies conceivable in the mind of Man.

For a time I was content to follow his footsteps through

127

the twists and turns and cul-de-sacs of the City, past bars and pawn shops and toy stores and tenements made of dried red bricks. The people we passed smiled discreetly — as if they, too, understood that Raine was close to finding whatever it was he had been seeking since before his departure from Earth. The Lazalites seemed to share in some joke to which Raine and I were oblivious, for their smiles were as much sinister as they were pitying.

We passed through shaded areas and hot blazing places where there were no eaves or trees, and where the sun scorched down to make transparent monkeys perform rain dances on the parched pavement. Children who were too young to attend school were playing in the streets, and their faces all seemed bright and knowing and utterly evil. They could have stopped us, could have warned us, yet they only continued with their very important play.

I damn them for that.

They knew Raine's answers before he knew them himself, yet they allowed him to continue on to his downfall like a man walking blindfolded toward a precipice. They played in the streets and congregated in alleyways to form circles where they would dance about one another until collapsing into near-spasmodic laughter on the red ground. And the laughter was of an unmistakably ironic nature. These children knew all there was to know about reality — about Raine and Crystal and the War on Terra and the end of the universe. Yet they could do nothing but smile their toothless smiles and whisper under their breath...

> "When Terrans came to sail dark seas
> And see what stars might be;
> Heaven moved with no forwarding address
> And left this void to me."

That is what they sang, that is what they whispered, that is what they knew. And it was, in some way, the only answer there would ever be. The mystery had gone out of space, the ancient gods had died, and the One True God had never sent his Son to any world other than Terra — and that only in legends whose truth or lie could not be validated.

And worst of all, even heaven had moved and left no forwarding address. Each of us and all of us is and ever shall be utterly alone.

*

I do not know precisely what it was that we had been expecting to find. We had called it, nebulously, The Answer. And yet, how did one know when one had found some mystical and intangible thing? It was perhaps the same as a saint receiving the stigmata or the Virgin Mary, if indeed she was ever more than a legend, receiving the seed of God during the Immaculate Conception.

In short, there was no way to know when one's mind was impregnated with truth.

That moment was never accompanied by throngs of cheering followers nor loud brass bands nor a signal from departed spirits. It existed as all other moments: insignificant save for the person who experienced it.

Perhaps that is why I did not even look up from the pale ochre dirt when Raine stopped walking that afternoon and took one of those deep breaths which signaled weariness or insight.

But it became apparent that Raine had reached the end of this particular road, and so I chanced a look at him. His dark eyes had turned almost pale brown in the brilliant sun of Lazali, and his expression was completely unreadable even to me. His thoughts, normally so open and warm, were altogether silent as he stared at something which seemed to hold him spellbound. I followed his gaze and tried not to shudder when one of those inexplicably cold winds came rolling through the deserted street in the middle of a Lazalite summer.

At the end of the cul-de-sac, Raine was staring at a plain brown building which leaned awkwardly to one side as if some mischievous spirit had dug up one corner and uprooted the foundation. It was the same brown, muddy substance as all the buildings in Semillon City, with dusty four-paned windows in the front and a wooden porch that had seen kinder times. The porch also leaned, but in the opposite direction as the tilt of the building itself, and a rotting wooden swing creaked an eerie melody on rusty chains that threatened to drop it at any moment.

But the thing which so mesmerized Raine was not the building. Instead, it was the sign hanging above the weathered door. It said quite simply and in Terran Standard:

Any Question Answered

Nothing more, nothing less. It could have been painted by a child in kindergarten, for the letters were awkwardly formed, and the cheap black enamel used to scribble the message was beginning to chip away so that only the most astute observer would bother to read it at all.

Raine looked at it for a long time, then at me, and then he started walking once more – up to the building that wavered and threatened to disappear in the heat, up to the door, up to his final answer.

I did not follow him, and what happened in that one-roomed haunted house came to me as Raine's nightmares had come to me through the decades – frightful and cold and filled with the sharp scent of doom.

*

Once inside the tiny room, Raine scanned the dusty furniture, some of which would have been very much at home in red brick buildings or abandoned antique stores back on

130

Terra. A single carved-back chair covered with fading green upholstery sat in one corner and was faced by a mismatched love seat. Two stools that had once been chairs, but had long since broken their spines and been reduced to backless monstrosities, leaned awkwardly against the wall.

The walls were the same muddy brown inside as outside – constructed of adobe-type clay that bubbled to the surface in Lazalite winters when rain was plentiful and the heat was not too vicious. The floor was made of planks – each one a different size. Some had started to buckle with stress, others had cracked entirely, and still others were completely missing, allowing the parched desert sand to show through in pale contrast to dark wood. Two four-paned windows boasted a year's worth of dirt and rocket soot and fingerprints, for in the summers water was too scarce to waste as a cleaning commodity.

Other than the chair, loveseat and the two stools, the room was devoid of furniture or any sign of an occupant. Raine stood there for a long time, studying the barren furnishings and wishing to all the nameless gods that he had never come here. A sensation of crawling scorpions hovered in his stomach, and even I could feel the devil's creatures maneuvering inside Raine from my waiting place outside.

Raine paced the plank floors for awhile, sat down, got up again, and even took a moment to draw a diagram of Terra in the soot on the window before finally abandoning his nervousness and settling down in the faded green chair to wait.

It wasn't until nightfall that his wait bore fruit. I did not see the young Lazalite woman enter the building, and were it not an entirely impossible notion, I might perceive that she had simply come into existence right there in the room with Raine. He had closed his eyes and drifted into a troubled meditation, but when he emerged from his half-trance, she was there – her eyes as black as his own, her hair falling below her slim waist in a straight shiny mass that resembled liquid onyx. She could have been no more than twenty five Terran years, this witch of Lazali, but Raine understood instantly that her wisdom must certainly span centuries. Her mind was quiet and ordered, and she wore one of those expressions the ancient monks of Earth must certainly have worn high in the secluded temples of China. She was at some sort of prearranged peace with the universe, with the forces of nature and gods, and with herself.

Raine studied her in silence for a time, his thoughts returning to Crystal, and to the differences and similarities between this Lazalite woman and his own beloved. In many ways, the witch was almost a perfect negative image of Crystal – dark-haired and dark-eyed and dark-minded. There was a familiarity surrounding her, and Raine found himself thinking of a house on Terra, a barn with the sweet scent of alfalfa hay, and the woman whom he had left behind.

And with that, perhaps Raine opened himself to her magic, and to his own end. With thoughts of love, he condemned himself, for if this sorceress could bring Raine his answers, he truly believed he would be able to return at last to Terra and home. In truth, however, he could no longer be certain if Crystal were even alive. Her letters had grown sparse and once Raine was presented with the physics of reality and time and space, he came to know that his own immortality had grown to be more of a curse than a blessing.

But he forced himself back to the only moment that truly existed. "I have come to have a question answered," he said. He normally did not speak in such straightforward terms, as Raine was an intentionally ambiguous and unintentionally romantic man whose speech was more comfortable with philosophical insights or poetry. But now he could not afford to be misunderstood, could not afford the luxury of verse or beauty or taxable happiness. Or perhaps he was already beginning to change.

The woman smiled, her straight white teeth perfect save for a crown of gold on one front incisor. It gave her the air of a pirate, or a flawed goddess who was no less perfect. It made her almost Terran, this familiar spirit of Lazali, but allowed her to retain the mystical air that seemed to permeate the air around her.

"I know why you have come here, Raine of Terra," she murmured as she took a seat by his side on one of those dilapidated chairs that gave a sigh of protest even against her slight weight. "You have come to ask me who you truly are – and why." Her dark eyes reflected the pastel colors of a Lazalite sunset as she inclined her head gently toward the window and the launchport beyond, and her expression became utterly sad.

"There is someone back on your Earth who can answer your questions far better than I," she continued, "and if you are as wise as your many years would indicate, you will return to her now – without ever asking your question."

She paused, studying Raine, photographing him with her eyes. "At this moment, it is not too late for you to go back – into your own past, if you wish, or into the past you once shared with your lover on Terra." But her eyes grew more stern as she spoke. "However, once you have asked your question, I will have no alternative but to give you the answers you seek. And truth is sometimes more of a jailer than a liberator."

Raine considered that for the briefest of moments. He was already possessed by this time – possessed by nothing more than a driving need to succeed. It is possible that it was not the answer which so infatuated Raine, but the question itself – *Who Am I?*

"Without answers, Man is void," he stated solemnly, his eyes locked with those of a woman who was both sorcerer and executioner. "Without knowledge of oneself, there can be no knowledge of others; without peace in oneself, there can be no lasting love."

The witch looked at Raine, and a faint and wistful smile came to visit her thin red lips. "You were not entirely at peace before, my Terran friend," she said knowingly and with painful accuracy, "and yet you have loved as few Earthers will ever love. You have loved the fields and the summer flowers and the scent of a beautiful woman in your arms. Is that not enough, even for a multitude of lifetimes?"

Raine shook his head – and oh how I damned him for that selfishness! It is possible that he was entranced by this woman, that her powers had blinded him even to his own mind or his own purpose, but I do not believe he could have been so easily mesmerized.

I should have gone inside at that moment, extracted him forcibly if necessary, and dragged him back to Terra. I would have sold my own soul to the devils of Lazalite sorcery if only I could have spared Raine. And yet... I could not move. I was a prisoner of the desert which surrounded me, as if some great pair of hands had reached up out of the clay beneath my feet and chained me to the floor less than twenty feet away from that haunted mud dwelling. I tell myself now that it was the witch's magic, that she is the demon who turned my legs to stone in that moment and in the hours which followed into madness. But in truth, I know it was my own inescapable fear.

"I must know," Raine stated, never realizing what he was giving up. "I must know of the woman who bore me and of the people who raised me, and of the world to which I truly belong."

The woman looked at him, through him, into him. "You are Terran," she stated after a few seconds, her tone leaving no room for doubt or argument. "So please – please go now. Accept that as your answer, for it is your truth. Do not bind me to continue, for there is a warning for you – a warning which has kept you safe for many years, but which will deliver up its power if you do not leave this world on the next transport and return to your home."

She pleaded with him for an hour, but Raine, like so many Terrans, was not content with the simplicity of truth. He was obsessed to hear the details, to see his own past, to relive whatever was so horrible that he had forgotten it to begin with. And though I had never witnessed that characteristic in Raine before, I thought of him as one of those faceless ghouls who appear on the scene of accidents and murders and utterly grotesque events. He had to *see* the things of his own past, his own accidents, his own murders which had taken place only in the nebulous landscape of his mind.

The sorceress could not sway him.

Finally, she looked at him one last time, as if to memorize the depth of feeling that still remained in his eyes, as if to put forever in her own memory the beauty of this creature whom she would be destined to destroy.

"Very well," she sighed at last. "Call me by my name of magic and ask your question, and I will be compelled to take you to your answers."

Raine met those dark eyes which were now twin reflections of his own. She was inside him and it only then dawned on him that he had not ever bothered to ask the witch her name, yet he knew it as well as he knew his own or mine.

"Tasme," he said in a voice that was suddenly very small and very much alone. "Who am I? Where am I to go, and why have I been compelled to leave Terra in search of those answers?"

At first, there was no reaction from either of them. Then, after a moment which could have been centuries, the love left Raine's eyes as all the worlds and all the galaxies became insignificant, and Reality ceased to exist in coherent form.

*

Shouting. Laughter. Release. Freedom.

White-clad nurses and grim-faced orderlies moving about corridors thick with the stench of the old and the dying and the peculiar odor that is indigenous only to the insane. A scent of stale lilac perfume and soiled bed sheets.

Bedlam. Chaos. Inmates of an asylum gone mad on a hot

135

summer night when the moon was almost full and stars were struggling to shine through a layer of soot and thunderheads. The sign on the nurses' station said:

BELLEVUE PSYCHIATRIC HOSPITAL

Raine looked down on it from above, down on the chaos and the madnesses which were more preposterous than ever before. He was a floating nonentity, drifting as a disembodied life form through florescent-lit corridors as doctors hurried to subdue violent patients and orderlies scrambled to lock the drug cabinets, and nurses tried to calm the frightened and sedate the frightening. Rape and violence. Seduction to the whispered lines of Shakespeare.

An old woman wearing a dirty bedpan on her head and reciting: "Romeo, Romeo? Wherefore art thou, Romeo?" as two inmates struggled and writhed and sweated and mated like animals on the sterile floor of the surgical suite.

Raine felt the darkness then, somewhere in the middle of rasping, breathing. He tasted the moment of life, the instant of his own conception, and the blackness became an enveloping sheath that held him close. But through the Lazalite witch's eyes, he remained disembodied and terrified, for this was his final answer, his utter truth, an illusion injected into the soul that could not be denied or swept away with some alien incantation. He observed the sordid mating which seemed to last an eternity, watched the woman with the bedpan on her head begin to applaud when Raine's father – an emaciated, wiry-haired sloth of a man who was blind in one eye – rolled off his mother and spilled the remainder of his stagnant seed onto the pale tile floor.

His mother, the Dark One among the graying and whitened faces, began to laugh, to clutch at her abdomen and proclaim that the seed of Lazarus was now deep inside her womb, and that new life would arise from Death when the satyr of ancient legends was birthed. She ran then, naked

136

through the corridors, slipping easily past the orderlies and doctors and nurses in the bedlam – for she was one of the Harmless Ones, one of those whose insanity had been passed on from generation to generation for centuries. She bore the Dark Seed – that scarring of genes and chromosomes that would ultimately bequeath her madness to any offspring. In another two days, she would have undergone the mandatory sterilization process, and yet Raine was within her even then. At first just a seed, a mass of biochemical's with no form and not yet large enough to be seen with the naked eye. But he lived.

The Dark One found a closet, donned a matron's uniform, then discovered an open door, a series of doors and corridors in the maze of the hospital, until finally she saw the pale, translucent glow of moonlight streaming in through the front entrance. She smiled warmly at the volunteers working the front desk, and they scarcely gave her a second glance as she walked out the confines of the asylum and into the arms of an even larger madhouse.

By the time the staff got around to comparing the number of patients with the number of beds, she had vanished into the city, swallowed up by skeletal stairwells and deserted flophouses and bars and flickering neon signs that pointed the way to anonymity among the masses.

Once outside the Treatment Center, Raine's mother became more sane than she had been during the six months of her confinement within those gray concrete walls. Perhaps, as Raine once suggested to me, insanity was not so much an ailment of genes and chromosomes or chemical imbalances in the blood, but an illness different from all other illnesses — for it had no genuine basis in reality. It was, therefore, a product of an individual mind – perhaps an extremely brilliant or extremely stupid individual who saw things more clearly than those of us who were considered to be sane. In short, Raine once said he believed insanity to be the precise opposite of its clinical definition, it was utter clarity of vision – both physical and psychic vision – and the "insane" were the only truly sane beings on Earth.

Raine felt that sanity was often a burden, and that only those souls who haunted asylums and donned dirty bedpans for hats and swatted at invisible flies would ever be free. They were free of time, free of War, free of financial burdens, and free of limitations.

At any rate, Raine's mother, whose name was actually Goldie, seemed to fall back into the lines of societal behavior once she had extracted herself from Bellevue.

With careful planning and a small measure of luck, she managed to find an unlocked boxcar, and by concealing herself in one of the crates labeled "Pillows and Linen", she was able to maintain passage all the way to the train's final destination – a small industrial city somewhere in the middle of the New Mexico desert. It seemed that the boxcar she had chosen was bound for one of the many communes out there – and when the crates were unloaded – with one crate being somewhat heavier than the rest – she discovered herself in the midst of a group of people who were genuinely pleased to have another convert. For in her madness, she found no difficulty in mimicking the void stares of the inhabitants of this commune. She was proficient at toiling the fields and eventually became as those of the colony already were – void.

She stayed with the Suppressionists for the months of her pregnancy, following the rules set forth in the commune for women who were bearing the future saviors of Terra. She wore the black cloak of penance even on the hottest of desert summer days, and allowed wires to be connected to her head while she slept, receiving the explanation that the child would come into the world with preprogrammed knowledge and insight. She learned the doctrine of Suppressionism, recited the rhetoric, and was soon indistinguishable from any of the other women in the Colony.

And on the night when Raine opted to be born, she went into the greenhouse, squatted underneath the air conditioning ducts and, without a cry of pain, without any feeling whatsoever (in accordance with the discipline of the Community), pushed the child from her body and onto the moist black dirt. The umbilical cord she cut with her own teeth, cuddled the dark child close until he began to breathe and murmur cooing sounds against her breast, then carefully laid him under the napa plants and fled from the Suppressionist colony and all the way back to Bellevue – where she announced that the Christ child had been born beneath a star in Bethlehem.

She would not however inform the doctors where this alleged Bethlehem was located, for they knew it was certainly not in the old city of biblical times. So no one at the hospital ever knew whether the offspring of Goldie's womb had lived or died. And, quite probably, not one of those doctors or nurses or orderlies or aides cared.

*

Raine then, was found in a cabbage patch, and perhaps that was the cold humor of Goldie's insane insight, her only legacy to him other than her madness.

*

The Suppressionists were pleased with the child despite his unorthodox birth — for he did not cry much even as an infant, and there was something decidedly peculiar about the dark eyes and gossamer ebony hair and the way he carried himself when he began to walk. He was, in essence, a very small adult — for that is how the Suppressionists wanted their children to be. He did not play with toy trucks or toy soldiers or build secret forts in secret places. Instead, he studied, learned, meditated and followed discipline.

Emotions, the Suppressionists taught, were the basis of humanity's problems. Therefore, according to Leu – the High

Master of the colony and founder of the doctrine – all feeling must be utterly banished from the moment of birth.

"In order to be free of hatred," Leu explained to Raine on the morning of his thirteenth birthday and the eve of his journey into manhood, "one must also be free of love. And to be free of love, one must be free of sexual needs. To be free of sexual needs, one must purge oneself of the demon of human desire."

And so on.

Leu, an Asian man who had been reared under the strictest of ancient disciplines, took upon himself the task of personally raising Raine, filling him with the philosophy of Suppressionism. In short, he gave himself the chore of altering all that was basic to Raine's personality. For Raine, even as a child, was filled with love. It shone through in his eyes on dark desert nights when a crescent moon hung low on a starry horizon, it radiated outward from him as heat from the sun, and it was eventually the cause of his first downfall.

The problem with the commune was that it had been founded solely by adults and had been in existence only a little over five years when Raine was born.

The children of those first five years were still in the experimental stage, and the adults – by *any* standards – were hardly rational. If they themselves had learned to hide and eventually destroy their own nature which made them human, they soon discovered that it was another matter entirely to teach their offspring to be as sterile-minded as they themselves had become. And when it became apparent that mere doctrine and discipline were not enough to purge a child's mind of the need for love and attention, they adopted harsher methods. Warmth or affection was rewarded by cold staring eyes and reproach. Anger was rewarded with banishment from the Colony for a day. Love was rewarded with hunger and isolation.

And, after a time Raine came to understand that he could not stay in the commune much longer. Some spark of

140

individuality remained alive in his mind, some fire burned and whispered that this was not the purpose of life. New horizons must certainly exist somewhere.

But Leu knew Raine's thoughts as well as he knew his own, and one night when the skies were pregnant with clouds and speaking of thunder, Leu went to Raine's tiny room as he slept and used the harshest discipline of all. He had once been a psychiatrist according to the old women of the Colony who had taken to answering some of Raine's questions, and the old man knew the values of mechanical intervention. He attached a device to Raine's head while he was asleep, and fed in all the proper impulses originally designed to calm violent patients in a psychiatric ward. Leu replaced what he took away with the correct Suppressionist responses, the proper mental attitude, the correct programming.

And what was left when it was over was the man Raine grew into – a man who had never known love and who had therefore never craved it. A man who had never hated and did not know how or why to hate. A man who had never desired a woman and who would never take a mate. What was left was Leu's image of perfection – a men devoid of all feelings, a man who would not go to War because he did not possess the hatred or jealousy or greed to want for anything more than his next breath. What was left when Leu was finished was a man who would never have the ability to love – for the memory of love's very existence had been sucked from his thoughts by a mechanical vampire while he slept.

*

The commune itself consisted of slightly more than fifty acres situated precisely in the unsurveyed center of Nowhere. Its perimeters were marked by a 10-foot chain link fence which, when viewed from the inside, broke the world into thousands of galvanized squares that fit together like pieces of a puzzle to form reality. It wasn't long before Raine became as

141

all the rest of the colonists – sterile in thought, barren of emotional response, and eventually something less than human. For it was these very emotions which Leu fought against so terribly, Raine later discovered, that gave man his ambition, his strength, his weakness and his purpose for existence. Without them, there was very little remaining. And yet, without them, there was no desire to seek another path. Contentment reigned in the void, leaving serenity, but also sterility.

But the Suppressionists were only one commune among hundreds that seemed to spring up out of the desert sands like some species of weed. They grew there for a time, but few flourished, and the majority were nothing more than weekly revivals that pulled up their tent stakes and vanished into the night after so short an existence. Rumor had it that the new colony "down the road" was made of up Expressionists — those who felt that the honest release of emotion was far more healthy than its suppression, and where orgies were supposedly encouraged and lynching of hitchhikers was a common means whereby to expel hate from the mind in the most primitive and natural of fashions.

But the Suppresionist Colony was self-sufficient, and since only Leu was permitted to travel beyond the locked fences, the validity of these rumors could never be determined. Whether they were only Leu's version of Hell, a fantasy to scare the Colonists into submission just as Hell had once been used to scare people into heaven, could not be verified. But by that time, most of the colonists were content and therefore entirely complacent. Whatever they had left behind was long since gone, and their only family consisted of the hollow stares of the people with whom they shared the commune.

Inside the fences, several buildings had been hastily thrown together, most constructed of scrap wood and shingles and tarpaper which made a most appropriate stage for the heat monkeys of summer. The structures were, for the most part, all identical – save for the large dining room/lecture hall

142

where the colonists were required to meet each evening to hear Leu explain the tenets in great and boring detail. Each night, when the heat had subsided to a tolerable level, and the workers were permitted to lay aside their shovels or hammers, the inhabitants would gather there, consume a bland diet of rice and vegetables, and privately wonder if Leu were as insane as his rhetoric started to sound once one had heard it a hundred times too often.

And yet, was it any different than any other belief system, injected into the minds of vulnerable subjects by zealots with an agenda? Believe in God. Trust the government. Fight for peace. All things die.

Not knowing *what* to believe, most people ended up believing what they were *told*, whether it had any basis in reality or not being altogether irrelevant.

The colonists were held together not so much by Leu, but by their own fears and doubts that could never be expressed. It was commonly (even if falsely) believed that everyone within the Colony's walls was there because his doctrine offered a better way of life than the lives which would have been available outside. In reality, no one left the Colony simply because no one *ever* had left the Colony – and all those no ones were perhaps too frightened to find out what would happen if they were caught, or worse, what might happen if they weren't. They were, therefore, prisoners of a doctrine, a series of lies, and fears unspoken and undefined. The fences could have been made of paper and would have held them just as tightly.

And Raine became part of those people, spending his days in the greenhouse tending the vegetables and fragile flowers that grew stubbornly between the rows, and wondering why he suddenly felt so empty and alone and meaningless, wondering why only Leu seemed three dimensional and alive.

Secretly Raine felt there was a man he had never known, a child he had never had the opportunity to be, yet when he attempted to remember those faces from his own past, he met with a black void darker than the space blood between galaxies – a void created by the surgical precision of Leu's machine. Even though it never broke the skin, it had broken the man.

Occasionally, Raine wondered if anyone else within the Colony had experienced these forbidden and punishable doubts, yet there was no way to find out. If one asked, and one was wrong...

And so the Colony consisted of the housing facilities, the toilet facilities, the dining hall and the greenhouse which was responsible for the majority of food and water upon which the colony depended. If Leu had originally brought his doctrines into this sterile desert in the belief that he could farm the land and coax water from the sky with a ritualistic dance, he was fated to dire disappointment. The soil was nothing more than parched sand and rains were scarce.

The only living thing outside the greenhouse was a single tree which Leu had brought with him from whatever life he had lived before. He had planted it in the desert sand as a reminder to the colonists that life and the continuation of life depended solely on discipline, and things could grow and flourish even in a barren climate – including the climate of a human mind that had been purged of all interfering feelings.

In reality, Leu spent much of his own time tending to the tree that had lost the majority of its leaves in the previous summer's heat, and was always starving for water, and often threatened to lay its branches on the ground and die when one of the windstorms came sneaking through the locked gates late in the evenings. Perhaps the tree was indeed the Colony's symbol, for its existence was a struggle and it seemed lonely in a world where it did not belong. It was displaced and utterly alone and melancholy without its own kind.

Yet Leu would not permit it to die.

Raine looked at the tree often, and thought of love – a word meaningless to him now, a word forbidden to utter, to think, to know. But he remembered the word, and continued to remember it until he was thirty, when Leu died one fine spring morning of nothing more spectacular than a cold, and the colonists who had not perished in the last season's flu epidemic held a funeral without tears or laughter or regret or sadness.

At Raine's suggestion, the old man was buried at the foot of his lonely tree. Once Leu was dead and the Colony found itself without a leader, few remained behind to tend the greenhouse or plant seeds in soil that would not nurse them to maturity. The majority of the colonists left as they had come to Leu's world, alone and with nothing. They left silently in the night – only a few at first, but in greater numbers as the fears subsided. And not one smiled or laughed or cried or experienced any sense of melancholy or joy to be leaving. It was a time period coming to its reasonable end, a passing into a new phase, a new beginning... and Raine found himself alone. Outside the colony's gates for the first tine in his life.

He traveled east for a period of days that were nothing more than a series of sunrises and sunsets across a gradually changing terrain. The red sands and the flat-top mesas slowly transformed into scrub desert and canyon lands. And the canyons turned into trees with no leaves and cacti which provided both food and water. And, finally, the cacti gave way to more trees, to swamplands and bogs, and the bogs were surrounded by tall and stately oaks and flanked by weeping willows who bowed their heads and sipped black water from cypress lakes teeming with life.

Though Raine had never seen any of these things before, he knew from his studies precisely what they were – down to the genus and species name of each. For the one thing Leu valued above the sterility of mind was knowledge. The children were taught geography and biology and zoology and all the computer sciences and maths – but none of Terran history. History was the one subject which had been absent from the Colony, for Leu believed that those who were students of the tragedies of history would always feel compelled to outdo them, to give something to the history books which would be worthy of note, such as a War. Raine, therefore knew precisely what chemicals and processes had gone into the making of the land and the trees and the motorized vehicles that zipped past him on freeways and winding country roads, but he knew absolutely nothing of their origin.

Yet the one thing which Raine knew how to do was something he did well, and upon reaching the outskirts of a small settlement in Louisiana, he happened upon a farmer who was short of hands, and who hired Raine immediately upon learning that he was well versed in the care of saplings and sprouts of all varieties. If the farmer ever considered him peculiar, Raine never knew of it, for as he quickly discovered, men did not seem to care much what their fellow humans did so long as they did it in privacy and did not attempt to force their beliefs or practices upon others.

In short, the farmer did not care whether Raine smiled at the blackbirds in the morning sky, nor whether he cried when one of the old mares was found dead in her stall one winter night. Raine was an efficient if quiet worker, and as long as his plants were sturdy and his fields were watered and his animals properly fed, the farmer did not seem to notice that Raine's eyes were devoid of all emotion, yet paradoxically filled with curiosity.

Raine was given food and lodging in a small guest house on the south side of the farm, and other than occasional trips into Wisner to purchase seeds and fertilizers, he spent his spare time studying from the old books he bought with his earnings, and listening to the educational radio station which broadcast from New Orleans each evening.

He learned history – of wars and threats of wars, and of men who killed out of lust and passion. He listened to the "drama" radio in the afternoon while he watered the fields, and learned again of love, albeit a rather peculiar brand of that particular emotion which was perhaps more idealized in radio

146

plays than in any reality. He studied fact and fiction, and everything he learned seemed to stay with him. If he was different than the other children at the Colony had been, it was perhaps due to Goldie and the wiry-haired sloth of a father who had created him. For though Raine did not know it at the time, both their IQ levels had been well over 160, forming the basis for Raine's intellectual abilities and his romanticism (which had been duly buried for nearly twenty years now), and for his ultimate insanities.

It has been said that the utterly brilliant are also cursed with utter romanticism or utter optimism or utter pessimism — and Raine was a precarious balance of all. Or, more precisely, he might have *been* a balance if he had not had the misfortune to fall asleep on that particular night when Leu had crept into his room and wiped his mind clean of all need for love.

Raine spent the next two years on the farm, and it wasn't until a particularly foreboding night in the middle of an orange autumn that he began to notice that he was indeed quite different from those who surrounded him. He had lived on an isolated farm after traveling from an isolated Colony of Suppressionists, and it wasn't until he was invited by the farmer and his wife to take a vacation "down South" (as they called Florida} that he came to recognize his own peculiarities. For though the farmer and his wife were certainly more emotional than Raine himself, Raine had never been a firsthand witness to "reality". He had never seen love demonstrated even in small ways – such as the way the farmer kissed his wife on the cheek each evening at the dinner table, or the way the farmer's wife stroked the kitten she had plucked from the barn cat's latest litter.

By the time the three of them had reached the Florida panhandle in the "Sunday driving car" – actually an old black Cadillac – the azaleas were in full pink-throated bloom and multicolored flox were peering out of the ground along roadsides where children played in apparent oblivion to passing automobiles and thundering trucks. They stopped for the night at a small motel, and the farmer even paid for Raine's private room, telling him that thinkers needed a place to think and, grinning at his wife, that lovers needed a place to love.

The motel was situated at the edge of a small creek which fed a river that eventually emptied into the Gulf of Mexico, and it was while Raine was walking in the late afternoon sun, almost daring to enjoy the feeling of warmth on his bare back, that he first noticed a thin breath of smoke rising up out of the forest that had completely swallowed him. The smoke appeared to dance above the azure forest like some legendary nymph must certainly have danced at ancient pagan weddings, and he found himself following it until he became hopelessly lost from the motel and the creek. He followed it for what seemed like miles, all the while watching tiny blue-striped lizards scurrying about the fallen leaves and squirrels skittering into hollow logs and mockingbirds involving themselves in peculiar mating dances in places where the sun had managed to sneak through a break in the thick leaves.

He traveled toward the smoke until he could smell its mysterious musk, its scent of autumn and dark earthtone colors and power. And when he stepped out from behind the trees into a small clearing is when he felt something stir in his mind which he had believed dead for years. For there, in an opening among the trees, was a group of people surrounding one dilapidated car, one van, and one surplus Army jeep that had seen better times. The people themselves wore brightly colored clothing; the women were sturdily built and dark, and the men were lean but powerful, with pale blue eyes set in tanned faces that showed no indication of age. The children – of which there were five – wore only ragged shorts with patches upon patches, and were dirty from having swum in the creek and later played in the loose Florida sand. Beyond the car and the jeep, the rusted-out van was backed in among the trees, and a makeshift tent had been slung between the

148

van and a towering oak which spread its branches over the flaps like some great bird of prey sheltering its young.

The children were dancing and laughing and playing with a piece of wood and a stone from the creek, batting it back and forth and running among the trees in some type of game which Raine did not immediately recognize. For though he had heard snatches of baseball games on the radio in Louisiana, he had never understood that children could play this same sport with makeshift equipment and healthy imaginations.

The three women were cloistered about the fire, apparently involved in cooking some elaborate concoction of potatoes, onions, carrots and other vegetables. Raine recognized the scent instantly from the farmer's house – when the farmer would toss what he referred to as "a little bit of everything" into a huge cast iron pot and boil it until the vegetables were tender and tiny opals of grease would settle on top of the brew as if to announce its readiness.

The two younger women seemed so young and vital, far more healthy than the female inhabitants of the Colony had been, and their tightly fitted jeans and low-necked blouses gave them the appearance of being surreal, like models from the brush of the old masters.

The youngest – whom Raine would later learn was called Jade – was stocky and strong, and when one of the children accidentally swatted the pebble against her leg, she turned, grabbed the youngster underneath his skinny arms and lifted him high into the air while laughing and scolding him in a peculiar manner which instantly bespoke love and compassion rather than any real disapproval.

When she released him, he scampered away and proceeded to do the same thing three additional times. It was as if the child craved the affection and the gentle discipline she gave to him, Raine thought. And though it was not particularly rational, and certainly not within the confines of the doctrines set forth at the Colony, he found himself wishing

149

he had known his own parents that intimately. Parents who would have laughed and scolded and spanked and cried, sang and rejoiced over nothing more exciting than a pot of vegetable soup.

There were also three men, and the two who weren't involved in unpacking brilliantly-colored blankets from the back of the van were plucking some alien-appearing instrument with six strings and a long neck that somehow reminded Raine of a swan. The young man began to play a melody in a minor key, and the voices of the two other scantily-clad men blended in perfect harmony as they related a legend of ancient England in song. They sang loud and strong, and though their voices were not of the same crisp and clear variety Raine had heard on the radio, they were nonetheless beautiful in some rugged way.

The words delivered up images of a beautiful woman and her secret lover who would scale ivy-covered walls each night to be with her regardless of the fact that she was betrothed to another. It conjured up images in Raine's mind of the Other Man – whom this woman did not love – and who eventually discovered her with her lover and slit their throats one night. And the lovers slept forever, buried side by side, and the ivy took nourishment from their bones and one day went to strangle her betrothed, who had come to mourn her death.

But Raine was perplexed. He had never quite understood what humans meant when they spoke of Death. Other than Leu's passing into another phase – which, according to doctrine, was the logical conclusion of any life form – he had not encountered it directly. At the Colony, there were occasional rumors of someone who had "passed" but Raine had always been encouraged to believe that this "passing" was only a moving beyond the gates of the Colony and into a larger world. Somewhere deep inside himself, he had known better. But his fear had held him mute and forced him to believe what he was told, as humans had been doing since the dawn of relentless time.

150

He had to know more. And with that as his sole excuse, he walked boldly into the clearing and stood gazing at the gypsies and their children who shared the forests with nature and smoke and autumn.

*

The moment he stepped into sight, the music drifted into silence and the children stopped playing and ran to their mother's side and all the world listened. Raine felt the tension immediately, for he had developed a certain talent at the Colony for being able to discern the moods, the unspoken feelings, even the thoughts of those around him. In an environment that prohibited natural expression, it was perhaps a natural mutation. He had communicated through telepathy with the kindly old woman who cooked beans and rice and with the retarded boy whom Leu had later "terminated."

He used it now – almost recklessly – for Raine was not then aware that his was a most special gift not shared by the majority of Terrans. He had the gift of mind-speak, the ability to project images and thoughts and pictures and sometimes even words into the minds of others, and at least one among the gypsies possessed the balanced ability to receive those images and understand those thoughts.

She was the one with pale green eyes and a face wrinkled and weathered with years. She was the one with loose-fitting clothes and a blue bandana tied about her graying hair. She was the one who had borne Jade, and whose name was Moira. She wore a red paisley print skirt which was gathered at the waist and which she hoisted in one hand as she moved toward Raine with utter confidence, motioning the men back down, for they had stood to defend the encampment from this intruder with black eyes and a muscled body out of folklore.

At her gesture they sat back down on the bumper of the jeep, and even the children resumed their play. Jade and her sister returned to stirring the soup, and only Moira seemed to possess any further interest in Raine at all.

She smiled, tilting her head curiously to one side as she approached him amidst the sunset colors of nightfall. Then, crossing strong arms across her chest, she stopped less than three feet in front of him.

"Either you smelled our food and are hungry, or else you are an answer to this old woman's prayers," she said in a lethargic accent. She cocked her head, waiting.

Raine studied her for a moment, at the same time studying the children who were dirty with sand and the two dark-haired sisters tending a pot of soup that could have cooked itself just as efficiently without their supervision. He glanced about the encampment, and felt the swell of forbidden emotions crawl to the surface once again.

He had heard of gypsies, but had considered them an extinct species. Yet here they were, like some illusion of spectacular beauty and peculiar customs that were as alien to Raine as the Colony had been. But here, at least, he felt at home, at peace, infatuated with a way of life he had never known – the life of a vagabond, the life of those who never stayed in one place long enough to see the change of the seasons or taste the fruit of their labor in the fields.

He had studied technicians who toiled over computers and mechanical things, he had learned of diplomats and presidents and ambassadors and warriors, he had come to understand the purpose of lawyers and cashiers and landlords and bagboys... but the gypsies were still a mystery to Raine. And it was that mystery which caused him to wonder, caused old Leu's restraints to waver, threatening to crash and leave him vulnerable to the emotions he had not experienced in a lifetime. He shivered in the afternoon warmth, thinking too many thoughts and feeling too many feelings for which he had no name or definition.

The old woman took another step forward, her gray brows narrowing as she put one hand carefully on his shoulder as if to steady him. But her smile gradually transformed to a frown as Raine flinched away, totally unaccustomed to the touch of another human being. He had grown used to the farmer slapping him on the shoulder in the morning, but that action, he surmised, was the farmer's way of expressing approval of Raine's work. It was intended for no purpose other than to circumvent the need for awkward "thank yous." And yet, when Moira touched him now, he knew that her touch was not meant as any sort of expression for something he had done. Instead, it was her way of knowing him, her way of coming inside his mind; and he quickly discovered that her thoughts were utterly alien to him.

Memories of campfires and sad, sad songs and sons who had been born and died without reaching maturity. There were memories of a husband who had run away in some dark Mississippi night with a younger and more attractive woman, thoughts and images and unshed tears and rippling quicksilver laughter and all those things Raine had been taught to believe were evil filled Moira's mind. And yet, they were soft and gentle and not so terrible after all.

He drew away, staggered backward a step, then stopped when the young man who had been arranging the blankets suddenly came over to stand by Moira's side.

"You must stay with us," the young man said in a voice that was clear and unbroken. "Allow Moira and me to heal the wounds which have been inflicted upon you."

Raine blinked, not understanding, for his body was the epitome of physical perfection. He had never so much as required stitches for foolish childhood accidents, for perhaps Raine had never been a child at all. He had never taken dares or run into unforgiving walls while chasing a ball, nor been careless enough to injure himself during his two years on the farm.

"I am not injured," he stated quietly, still looking at the man who resembled one of the men he had known at the Colony, one who was his same age... one he would never see

153

again.

But the gypsy shook his head and gave a warm smile that took Raine off guard. "It is not your body of which I speak," he clarified, deep eyes scanning Raine's entire being. "It is your mind, my friend, where the damage has been done, it is your thoughts that must be soothed and calmed and sorted before you can leave us." As he smiled, Moira also smiled, and even Jade turned from her soup to sigh in what might have been relief as she, too, nodded very slightly in Raine's direction.

"Yes," Moira quickly agreed, grasping Raine firmly by one arm and leading him over to sit by her on the bumper of the old green jalopy which was covered with the dust and mud of a dozen states. "You must remain with us for a time, my young friend, and learn what it is to be a gypsy – learn what it is for your lips part in song, what it is to know the joy of a woman and the warmth of a brother." She smiled more broadly, revealing teeth which sparkled with gold and silver crowns. "You must learn what it is to love," she said then, and clasped Raine's hand firmly between her own.

Raine lifted his eyes to stare at the old woman with something bordering on fear – not of the woman herself, but of the blasphemy that came so casually from her lips.

"But is not love something that must be abandoned in order to abandon hatred?" he wondered aloud, still finding it difficult to believe that people anywhere could speak so carelessly. On the radio, it was accepted. In fiction and in books, it was accepted... but in reality?

But before he could ponder it further, the old gypsy woman threw her head back and began to laugh, and gradually the others followed suit – from Jade to the children to the three men now standing in a semicircle facing Raine.

"Gypsies own no property, my friend," she said, "and there has never been a war in our ranks. Yet we are reputed by those who envy us and those who fear us to be the very instigators and perpetrators of all the love which has ever been or ever will be." She laughed again despite Raine's

154

perplexed expression, and impulsively pulled him tight to her chest and kissed him once on each cheek, hugging him, rubbing his back briskly.

But Raine remained as hard and cold as a granite boulder, neither responding nor deflecting her affection. Something in him wanted to accept it, to banish Leu's teachings forever from his mind, but another part of him that was still an obedient child would not permit it.

And Moira's eyes darkened for a moment with compassion. "You are a gypsy now, my dark-eyed friend," she explained, as if that should send all the fears and reservations back into oblivion. "You are a gypsy boy who will learn what it is to be warm inside, what it is to be sad... and, most of all, what it is to be loved."

She glanced briefly at the young man who had spoken to Raine a few moments before, then gestured him forward. When he stood by her side, she grasped his hand – which was covered with elaborate gold and silver rings – and placed it in Raine's, urging their fingers to entwine in some ritual that was meaningless to Raine, but which obviously held some deep significance for her.

"My son will come into your mind while you sleep tonight, " she continued, holding their hands together and joining them in some mystical fashion. "He will show you those feelings which have been sucked from your marrow, and he will teach you how to reconstruct the damaged portions of your mind." She hugged her son closer to one side, then kissed him tenderly on the cheek.

"For you see, Fogg is the healer of our kind – and he is as enamored of love as you once were... and will one day be again."

*

For a single instant, I thought the Lazalite witch had thrown in some of her own magic – a magic that had reached beyond the adobe walls of her castle and out to where I was still standing dumbfounded in the sand-whipped streets. For the barest of moments, I thought she was merely manufacturing this mind illusion for the purpose of confusing Raine and myself, and perhaps as some form of amusement for herself. And yet, as I looked at the scene still captured in Raine's mind, I saw that the young gypsy man was indeed a reflection of myself. And it was not difficult to see why I was different. As an empath even then, I was constrained to be what the gypsies were – dark and mysterious and free in mind and spirit.

And so, in Raine's discovering his answers, I found that my own were irrefutably connected. Perhaps that is why he seemed so familiar to me that day I saw him at the edge of an orange grove in Florida, and perhaps that is why we seemed to circle one another for years without ever knowing it consciously, and why we were inevitably drawn to this world on the edge of a galaxy gone amuck.

At that moment, it might not have been too late to put an end to the insane quest for answers, yet I was now as obsessed as Raine had become. I could no more run into that mud-brick building and retrieve him than I could have slit my own wrists and watch my blood drip onto the anonymous sands of Lazali.

Time became a nonentity, and I do not know if I stood there for another ten minutes or another ten years, but I do not believe it would have mattered either way. Already, the magic of the past was dissipating, the spell was shattered, and the colors of doom and infinity were clearly painted in the too-bright night sky.

*

Raine spent the next six months traveling with Moira, Fogg and the gypsies. (I shall refer to Fogg in the third person, since he seems so utterly different than the man I have become since leaving that tiny band of Terrans, and in order to be objective about the events which transpired, perhaps it is best not to involve myself personally).

They took the jeep and the van and the car which squeaked and complained as it was driven, and made their way across the countryside, stopping each night in some secluded corner of reality to pitch a ragged tent under a sky filled with thousands of curious golden eyes. Fogg remained by Raine's side constantly, using his empathic ability to take the void of non-emotion into himself, replacing it with simple human affection. And yet, as Fogg discovered, attempting to explain love to a man who had never known it was perhaps even more difficult than attempting to describe the flavor of squid to someone who had never eaten it. For Leu's doctrines were imbedded deeply – *too* deeply to be removed with mental surgery or telepathic warmth or even cold sterile explanations, which Raine seemed to understand, but which had no genuine basis in reality for him.

Their travels took them from the swamplands of Florida to the tenements of New York to the deserts of Arizona and New Mexico, where Raine seemed to feel quite at home. And perhaps there was some melancholy significance to that fact. Raine, a man devoid of feeling, was more at home in the barren and utterly dead terrain of the desert than he had been in the bustle of life in New York or among the trees and flowers and lakes rippling with life in Florida. He was more comfortable in a climate where nothing grew and all was wasteland and even the skies would not relinquish life-giving water to the creatures below. Raine seemed to thrive there – but despite the heat of the sun and the scorching sands, the desert was an utterly cold place to Fogg and to the gypsies. Only Raine seemed not to notice that the desert was a place intended for communes and dune buggies and things which do not really live.

By this time, the economy of the "real" world had fallen into bad times, and rumors reached even the most secluded corners. There were whispers of a war, of conflicts in the Middle East, and of soldiers in training for battle. There were stories of unemployment and dramatic rises in crime and children who were put up for adoption because their parents could no longer afford to feed and clothe them.

And Raine did not *want* to love once he heard these rumors, for Leu's evil was still strong enough in his mind that he still sometimes perceived love and all emotions to be the *cause* behind these rumors. If love did not exist, greed would not exist, there would be no jealousy over resources and lands, there would be no wars.

It was during one of those long nights in the desert, when Fogg was attempting to heal the scars in Raine's mind, and Rachael and Jade were cooking the nightly pot of stew, and Jared and Desmond were singing sad songs to the stars that Moira went alone into the desert and did not return for two days. There was no sense of panic or in her disappearance, for the gypsies had learned through the years that solitude was often a necessary burden for the Mind-mother, and if she never returned, it was because she had made her peace with the forces in the universe and had found a cool place among the rocks to die. Even the children scarcely noticed that she was gone.

When she did return, Desmond composed a new song, Jared sang it – slightly offkey – and Jade watched her mother for a very long time that evening. There was a sadness and a determination in the old gypsy's eyes, and Jade understood that the old ways of magic which had not been practiced in over a century would have to be used once again. For Jade had learned to love Raine more deeply than she loved the vegetables and the flowers and the silver-bright sky of morning. She loved him more deeply than the vagabond's life, and her own sympathetic magic had gone with Moira into that desert night which lasted two complete days.

Moira, upon her return from the desert, came upon Fogg and Raine slightly less than half a mile from the actual encampment. Raine glanced up and thought for a moment that she made a striking silhouette against the pale sands that seemed yellow in the moonlight. But he quickly blinked the romantic notion from his mind, as he had been taught at the Colony.

Fogg had shown him how to appreciate the beauty of the land, the scent of a flower, the taste of well prepared foods. But Raine's appreciation of those was not a danger, for there was no particular crime in liking those things which could not return his affections. It was safe to admire the sight of the dunes in the nights, and to marvel at the smell of heat dissipating upon the smooth granite boulders in the early evening. The stark silhouette which was Moira must not be appreciated. She must be seen and analyzed only, all else bordered on sacrilege. And if he came to love her and her beautiful daughter, he would feel a need to protect them. And if he felt that need, he would learn to kill in order to keep them safe. And so the syndrome would play out as it always did, escalating as it always had, until it would be out of hand and out of control.

When Moira reached them, Raine looked up into the shadowed face as she knelt by their sides.

"You have been with us for many months, Raine," she said, her voice suddenly much younger than it had sounded in the days before.

He wished that he could see her face, for there seemed to be something different about her. He envisioned a beautiful young gypsy woman whose features were not weathered and old, but whose natural splendor would have been a danger even to old Leu himself. He blinked once, attempting to send the irrational image away.

"Yes, Moira," he agreed at last, glancing out the corner of his eye to Fogg, who was carefully braiding the frayed ends of a bandana together then unbraiding them, only to repeat the process endlessly. "I have learned much and hope to learn more." But he could not look at Moira, instead, he continued to watch Fogg, attempting to decipher the peculiar action which served no purpose.

Finally, when there was only silence and darkness, he looked up to see Moira's dark eyes catch a stray beam of moonlight and reflect it back to the sky.

"You have learned our ways well, Raine," she stated quietly, "but you still have not learned what it means to be a gypsy. You have learned to take what you need to survive and which cannot be bought with coins, you have learned to play the mandolin and sing songs to the night. You have learned not to value the things which no man can own..."

Here her voice softened, and Raine knew that what she said next would somehow change his destiny forever.

"And yet you have learned nothing at all – for you have not yet learned what it is to love as all gypsies love," she said at last, and even the crickets stopped singing and all the world fell into a terrible silence.

Not wanting to believe her, yet feeling the depth of truth all the way through to his soul, Raine blinked once again, struggling not to succumb to the overwhelming sense of sadness that seemed to grab him and shake him from the inside out.

He glanced at Fogg, and reached out to grasp his gypsy brother's hand firmly, forcing the other man to look up. "I have learned that love is something which must be experienced through the eyes of a child, Mother," Raine said, for all the gypsies of all the tribes called Moira 'mother'. "As a child, love was merely an illusion to me, but I have come to know that it is not something that can be taught or learned." His words sounded hollow, even to his own ears.

Moira spat upon the ground. "We gypsies have another saying – one you may not understand, but which is nonetheless relevant to your way of thinking, my new son. Would you like to hear it?"

Raine nodded, for he never tired of the legends and myths and obscure statements that seemed to flow with such ease from Moira's mouth. "Yes, Mother," he replied reverently. "I would be interested in your thoughts on this matter."

She sat down on the cool desert ground, and reached out to grasp one of Raine's hands on one side, and one of Fogg's on the other, completing their tiny circle. Then, as if all were right with the world, she released a sigh which had been building for days. "Though you state it in mighty terms, Raine, what you are saying is that one cannot teach an old dog new tricks."

Raine stared at her, then at Fogg, who seemed to be smiling wistfully in the middle of the surrounding darkness. "I do not understand," he said truthfully.

Moira sighed once more, squeezing his hand more tightly. "Poor, poor boy," she said with a shake of her head that caused moonglow to glint off her long grey hair. "You've got it in your head that you can't love simply because some old man once told you that love is a sin. In essence, my dear child," she continued in her thick gypsy accent, "you're hooked on *religion*."

Raine stared at her without really seeing her. "Religion is a fallacy," he said, recalling what he had learned at the Colony, "for there is no One True God. There are only forces of nature and forces of Man and the interaction of the two which occasionally combine to produce peculiar phenomena not comprehensible by Man."

Moira laughed lightly. "So insightful you are, little one. Yet, for all your knowledge and all your inner brightness, you cannot see your own self-imposed limitations." She looked him squarely in the eye and held his hand as if in some ancient ritualistic fashion. "Are you *happy*?" she asked pointedly.

Raine did not respond at first — partially because this was a question he had never considered in such blunt terms. The farmer's wife had hinted at it on occasion, but he had passed it off as mere curiosity and had not considered it any further. Finally, he broke the eye contact with Moira (which was suddenly far too probing) and looked instead at Fogg.

"I am content," he decided aloud. "I am content to know that I shall never be the cause of a war, nor shall I ever kill a man out of lust. And if that constitutes happiness, then—"

Moira cut him off with a squeeze of his hand and a gentle smile he did not permit himself to see. "It does not, my boy. It does *not* at all make a recipe for happiness." She paused for a moment, wetting her lips against the cold, dry wind of the desert, then continued. "Just the opposite, I suspect. Contentment is the *lack* of happiness, the *absence* of all the gypsies worship and call into being." At last, she made him look at her again, with nothing more than a casual thought placed in his mind. "And you are after all, more of a true gypsy than any of us."

Raine looked into her eyes, into the dark irises and pale brown pupils. "Why?" he wondered, holding tighter to Fogg almost unconsciously. "What do you say such a thing?"

Moira smiled very gently and bent to kiss him lightly on the cheek. "There are so many paths a man can travel," she explained. "There are lines in your mind that are roads, and some of us who pay little attention to what is known as worldly reality have learned to decipher those lines."

She paused, studying him silently for a moment before continuing. "You may wish to scoff and deem it nothing more than magic, but such will be your downfall if you do not listen to me and to Fogg. You have simply been placed on the wrong road by a man who sought to control you for his own purposes – which is the legacy of all cults and most religions when you really stop to look at it.

"You have been guided down the wrong path in your mind, for it is not your true nature to be such a cold and unfeeling creature." She ran her fingertip along the lines in Raine's palm, but he scarcely seemed to notice. "Your mind is greater than any of us who surround you. Yet as long as you are locked *inside* that mind, you will never be free. So long as you are compelled to be nothing more than what you are in

162

this one moment, you will not grow. Just as dormant seed will lie forever in the skin of the Earth, so will you lie forever in the potential of what you may be instead of ever really Becoming."

And Raine, for a single instant, felt utterly sad. Perhaps that was the beginning of his change, perhaps that is when someone – for the first time – defined the core of what Raine was. He had been, up until that time, a prisoner of Leu's doctrine, a slave to Leu's treatments, a sheep content to blindly walk to slaughter without so much as a cry of protest.

"And yet," he said, his voice becoming deeper and sadder as a faint breeze blew across his face, "I cannot be other than what I am. I cannot abandon all I have been to become that which I do not know—"

"Fear," Moira said, "is the only bar on your prison, my boy. Lose that bondage, open your thoughts to nothing more spectacular than gypsy magic, and you will learn that you are wrong." She hesitated for a moment, as if considering whether or not to continue. Then, at last, she pulled Raine tight against her chest. "Tell me," she whispered close to his ear, "do you want to understand the things you do not know? Do you *want* to love?"

Raine looked at the ground over Moira's shoulder, and tried not to be touched by the feelings of compassion and unfamiliar emotions that washed in on him from the old gypsy's mind. He closed his eyes, and pretended that the moisture in them was nothing more than dew.

"Do not be afraid," she encouraged gently. "For Fogg will be with you always, and by freeing yourself, perhaps you can free him as well."

Raine glanced up sharply, first at Moira, then at Fogg. "I do not understand," he murmured once more. "For surely Fogg is as free as—"

Moira gazed at Fogg as Raine's voice drifted into silence. "Fogg is perhaps the opposite of what you are, my friend," she explained sadly. "For it was his destiny in this life to walk down the road of an empath – one who cannot help but love and hate and fear and dread and desire that which he can never have."

She sighed, and Raine thought for a moment that he felt Fogg slip a little further away from him. He did not comprehend embarrassment, but the sudden emptiness left him cold, even lonely.

"Fogg is a beloved gypsy," Moira explained, "as well as a healer. But he will never be a husband or a father, for he will always be nothing but a reflection of those around him." She grasped Raine's hand more tightly, and looked at both her sons. "Free him," she pleaded. "If you are afraid to free yourself, then please let him go."

Raine stared at Fogg, at the frightened eyes set deep in a richly tanned ageless face. He thought of the times they had spent together, of the long walks in places with no name, and the times when Fogg had struggled so terribly to explain love to him. But now... as he really looked at Fogg, he saw the other prisoner – the prisoner *he* had created. For Fogg was no longer capable of knowing love either. He was a mirror of Raine himself – a mirror that could not change direction of its own accord or point itself toward a more acceptable light source.

Raine turned his eyes back to Moira after a very long time and felt something tear free inside himself. "Tell me of your magic, Mother," he said quietly. "Tell me of childhood and make me understand what it is to love." He looked at Fogg one last time. "For I cannot be content to steal another man's life."

Moira looked first to Fogg, then to Raine, and finally down at the ground in the center of their circle, and for a moment, it seemed as if she might reconsider the entire matter, walk back to the encampment where the children were arguing over a newly found lizard, and go to sleep in her blankets underneath a ragged canopy that permitted the stars to shine through. But the reservations gradually left her eyes as she reached down to unstrap a flask of liquid which was always on her bright silver cloth belt.

"Do you believe in magic, Raine?" she asked almost jokingly.

Raine shook his head, but Moira only continued to smile.

"No matter," she said, pulling the cork from the ancient green bottle and taking a moment to smell the contents. "For this isn't truly magic, at least not in the ancient sense of the word." She grinned broadly, revealing the gold and silver in her teeth. "It's science, Raine, and maybe that will make it a little easier for you to comprehend."

Raine looked at the bottle with something bordering on dismay, and he thought of the legends he had learned on his radio back in Louisiana. Legends and myths and lies with no basis in fact or reality. Love potions. Potions to heal. Potions to kill. Potions to counteract other potions...

Surely Moira was more than that, he thought desperately. Surely she would not resort to the tactics of faith healers who did nothing more than activate their "patient's" own mental abilities through trickery. Surely, he thought, Moira would not do this to him and expect him to believe it.

And yet, as he looked at the green bottle, he thought he saw something most peculiar. The glass seemed to shift shape in the pale moonlight... or perhaps that, too, was nothing more than illusion created by fatigue and guilt. He thought of Fogg once again, of how he had doomed his gypsy brother to be what he himself already was: a being incapable genuine human feeling. He thought of how Fogg had been so full of life when they had first met, how the gypsy boy had laughed and danced so freely and easily. But now, Fogg sat by his side, solemn and cold and utterly quiet of mind and devoid of passion.

The guilt came back, tangible and cold and silver-deadly. And Raine stared at the bottle – the way it reflected light like a mirror, at the contents which appeared to be darker than the glass itself. For a moment, he wondered if he was about to drink nothing more than mud and toad urine, but he quickly passed that thought to the back of his mind. Fogg must be free again, he thought and the price seemed a fair one.

Moira studied her concoction for a long time, then sat it down in the middle of the circle. She grasped Raine's hand once again, turned it palm up, and before he knew precisely what was transpiring, she had pulled a gold-handled knife from somewhere in her blouse and made a quick incision in the shape of a crescent moon in the exact center of his palm.

He did not flinch, did not cry out despite the fact that the cut was deep. Regardless of his attempts to block the nerve impulses to the brain, the throbbing increased, reminding him of illusion and fantasy and reality and the intersect point between the three. He watched disjointedly as the old gypsy woman made an identical cut in the palm of Fogg's hand, watched Fogg stare at the blood of his ancestors in apparent fascination while some forlorn night bird went screeching across the sky as if to flee from the insanity which had come to live in her desert.

"Tell me what you feel?" Moira asked, her accent thicker with the scent of blood on the air. "Tell me of the pain."

Raine started to speak, and realized with purely objective fascination that he was staring directly into Fogg's mind. More than his eyes, he was inside Fogg's thoughts. Their voice came out as a harmony, for they spoke the same words in accurate unison.

"Pain is the absence of all other sensations," they murmured. "Pain is the obstruction of all save itself."

Moira nodded almost to herself, and saw two drops of blood mingle in the sand where they would be forever lost. "There is a danger," she warned Raine. "There is a danger of going further – for if you are to become what you were meant to be, you must lose and forget forever that which you have been." She met his eyes as another drop of his blood was forfeit to the desert. "Do you understand me? Do you understand that, by accepting gypsy magic, you will be forever forsaking the man you have known?"

Raine was entranced then, like a man who has imbibed too much liquor, or who had just witnessed the birth of all the nameless gods of the galaxy. "I understand, Mother," he said in harmony with Fogg's voice. "*I-who-am-we* understand."

But Moira leaned closer and tilted Raine's palm up to the stars. "There will be questions to be answered as time passes by you, my children," she whispered, "and you must understand one thing: If you ever discover the man who has walked your path before this night – if you ever seek to know who you were before this moment, you will be doomed to return to the path that man once followed.

"If you accept the gift of love as you have accepted the gift of pain, you must be forever one with a new path. You must *never* attempt to reunite with your past." Her voice sounded small and cracked with years which were not entirely her own. "You can never go back, my children. Do you understand that?"

Raine nodded and noticed that he could not close his eyes. He was staring at the blood on his palm, at the blood which was his past draining out of him. Already, Leu's Colony was little more than a nightmare, a dream that had come in the darkness and was already fading with the gradual coming of morning.

For myself , though I was present at the time of the event, I have no memory of the things which transpired, save for those images I have seen in Raine's mind as a result of Lazalite sorcery.

I do not want answers any longer.

Moira became the only reality – Moira and Fogg and the blood that was dripping more slowly onto the ground. It was his past, Raine realized. His blood was Leu, and Goldie's madness, and the farmer's wife and the vegetable soup and all that had gone before. And he realized with a sudden clarity of vision that he was not giving up very much at all. He was giving up nothing more than a series of memories taken out of context which had formed the basis of his reality. He was giving up nothing tangible or intangible, for he had had nothing until that moment.

The only sadness came with the knowledge that he must leave the gypsies forever – for they, too, were part of the man who had traveled another road. He must put them into his blood and leave them in the desert and nevermore return to their way of life. Only Fogg would be with him, and they would be as infants in a new world.

He looked up once, and saw a single line of tears on Moira's round cheeks. She was crying, perhaps in joy or perhaps in melancholy, for two sons who would be sons no more. She was crying for the children who would grow and eventually choose their own roads as well. And she was crying for the utter futility of life itself – that short span of time allotted to humans during which they must either succeed or fail at one thing or another... and none of it would make any difference in a thousand years.

"I understand, Mother," Raine whispered, and let his own tears spill over at last, falling at the same rate Fogg's were falling.

He tasted Fogg's sadness, his gypsy love, his empathy with all things that lived and breathed and were more alive than Raine had ever been. Together, they cried for the Mother they were losing, for the blackness they were facing, for the uncertainty of the future which was the only certainty at all now.

Raine was vaguely aware of Moira joining their hands once again, and of the different texture and temperature of Fogg's blood as their slashed palms met. He closed his eyes, but he was not blinded. Instead, he *saw* Moira pour the contents of the green bottle over their clasped hands, he *saw* the last of her tears mingle and mate with the blood in the sands.

Not magic... but science.

Raine heard the words through a distant tunnel that was

filled with whispering wind and murmuring memories that were already starting to fade, and with utter silence that was all that remained once it was over. Perhaps it was indeed science. He had learned of potions that could selectively blot out memories too painful to bear, and though the Amnesia Merchants had not yet been commercially manufactured when Moira sent Raine and Fogg into a dark slumber on that night in the desert, perhaps her potion was no less scientific than those.

Raine looked at the receding memories one last time, settling on an image of Leu. He saw the old man through different eyes, for he was already changing, mutating, becoming something he had never been. He saw Leu and himself, and realized they had not been very different after all. Leu had merely chosen the wrong path, but there were no gypsies to make him forget and allow him to live and show him that love was not such an evil concept after all.

He closed his psychic eyes then, and left them closed until morning, and when he awoke, it was to discover himself alone. He looked down and studied himself for the first time, and if he noticed places in the sand where two friends had once sat, he paid no attention. He was as a child abandoned in the desert, yet he was unafraid. He looked up at the morning sky and felt something that had been a name go fluttering like quicksilver through his veins.

He felt *love* – and a need for it which would make him immortal. That was Moira's legacy, though he could not understand it at the time. For her science was also a form of sorcery, and she had given him something only the gypsies had had before: eternal life and eternal love and a spell that must not be broken with answers or questions or any other human intervention.

She gave him magic, and he set off in the desert to find a highway which would lead to another part of the world, and would eventually lead to Aralin. And Aralin would lead to grief – which Raine would discover was a bittersweet mistress

– and grief would, in the end, lead to the search for renewed love. And that search would lead to Crystal Raine's beloved who could not hold him once he began to grow once more.

And therein, I discovered, lay the fallacy of the magic. For, as Moira had stated, no man could forever remain as he was in any given moment. Change was the only constant and questions the ultimate poison while paradoxically the only truly unrelenting part of Man's nature.

And answers, for all their practical or intangible value, were the final liberator of Love. Raine was finally free of it – all of it... in a tiny room on a secluded world where a witch had taken his mind into the past, Raine was free of his love.

And all that remained were the answers, cold and sterile. And, when viewed in the harsh perspective of life itself, terribly unimportant.

For a very long time which might have been no more than a nanosecond, I remained standing outside in the now dark streets of Semillon City. The spell was broken — both the spell of the Lazalite witch, and the spell of the old gypsy woman back on Terra. And magic, therefore, was a never-ending circle. Its ultimate power rested in the hands of the most accomplished magician, and Tasme had, against even her own wishes, taken away from Raine that which he had treasured so dearly – his ability to love and to be loved in return and to appreciate the beauty of fragile and transient things.

When I discovered that I could move again, I walked slowly up the stone path and into the room which depended on one half-burned white candle for its only source of light. Tasme was gone, and only the flickering shadows and the faint scent which is indigenous to a witch remained to remind Raine that she had existed.

He sat alone in the pale green chair which was covered with rocket soot and dirty fingerprints and reeked with memories and tears of those who had sat in it before.

I had hoped that Moira's magic or science or power had been stronger than the curse of Raine's past, but the moment

170

our eyes met in dull yellow shadows I knew I had lost him –
or, at the very least, I had lost the person I had come to know
over the years we had spent together.

I do not know what became of me during the time
immediately following the casting of Moira's spell, and during
the time Raine spent with Aralin. But I suspect I was
somewhere amidst the huge anonymous rocks of the desert
adjusting to whatever changes had come within myself. I
know only that the love which had been in Raine's eyes the
night Moira liberated him was now obliterated, and I felt the
dawning emptiness within my own mind as well. Like blood
being sucked from the veins. Like wine poured away. Like
leaves which had fallen in autumn and crumbled to dust. I
now faced the former Raine once again as we met again at that
old intersection in the road.

"There is a transport which leaves for Terra by the first
light of morning," I suggested, feeling my voice quaver with
fear.

But Raine only shook his head, and I saw in those black
eyes a raw pain which I had never before witnessed. For even
though Raine was now returned to the man he had been after
leaving Leu's Colony, he still maintained his *memories* of love ,
and perhaps that was the cruelest irony of all. Like a man
whose legs had been chopped off could recall the pleasure of
running through dew-covered fields in the morning, Raine
still possessed the vivid memories of Aralin's soft beauty, of
Crystal's tender acceptance, or Miguel's hesitant embrace. And
it hurt to remember how it had felt to be held in some dark
night when the clouds were talking of rain and brilliant
flashes of summer lightning pointed the way to Terra with
jagged white fingers. He had all those memories, yet was
totally incapable of responding to them. They were stored
facts, old data, bars on the prison.

"There is nothing on Terra for us now, my friend," he said
at last, but his voice was hollow and cold and utterly without
feeling. He could not even mourn his losses. "There is nothing

on Terra save a woman who would not know me and a life among the ruins." He turned those dark eyes on me once again, and I felt myself shiver. "Leu was correct," he said, and I felt the last tear slide down my own cheek. I had dared to hope I was wrong. I had prayed to nameless and uninterested deities that Raine's own mind would be powerful enough to sustain the magic even though he had trespassed into the territory of the warning.

"Yes..." he mused "Leu was indeed correct – for one cannot ever hope to *keep* love, and intangible things are the most fleeting of all."

Intangible things. That is all love ever really was or would ever be for anyone. At least that is what Raine believed in that fatal, final analysis.

"What will you do?" I wondered, listening to the floorboards creak with nightfall and the expansion of cooling molecules. "What will become of you?"

He was silent for a very long time as he placed one hand thoughtfully to his forehead and pondered the peculiarity of his own behavior – past, present and future. Outside the dust-covered windows, rockets were coming and going, oblivious to the event which had happened on this lonely world, and a few bold stars peered curiously through the soot and whirling sands as if to see what changes had transpired. In the distance, a neon sign flickered high above the city, its moving arrow pointing down at the business district which was filled with bars and tramps and winos and children who had all the answers they would ever need.

I envied them.

Raine took a deep breath, breaking the glassy silence, and I wondered if he would respond to my question at all. He rose from the chair like a man resurrected after electrocution, and walked to that window to stare at the tiny points of light. But he was dead inside... dead and buried and utterly alone.

"There are other gypsies somewhere, my friend," he said to me. "On all the worlds we have visited... surely there are

172

other gypsies."

Very slowly, he released the long breath, and continued staring at the rockets and the launchpad and the city and the stillness. Somewhere, perhaps in a nearby building, an old woman was coughing and a radio was blaring out its commercial messages into the empty streets and cold dark alleyways.

"It is only a matter of time before..."

He fell silent then, his broad shoulders seeming to slump in defeat as a rocket pirouetted in the sky with the grace of some cosmic ballet dancer then disappeared with a trail of orange laughter into ebony-blooded blackness.

"A matter of time?" I wondered, feeling lost and cold and frightened.

Raine nodded, but did not elaborate. "You will go with me?" he asked very quietly, inclining his head upward, toward the stars.

Without thinking, I slowly murmured my agreement. But even that seemed so empty, so final, and I was not at all certain that a spell, once broken, could ever be reinstated.

"I am sorry, my friend," I whispered to Raine. "I am so *very* sorry."

But I placed one hand on his shoulder and let my sorrow go with the departing rockets bound for Terra. It seemed, then, that Raine was nothing more or less than any other man. He was not some progeny of the stars as he had once fancied himself to be, nor was he altogether sane. Few men were. I knew that, as an empath, I could not hope to remain aloof from Raine's thoughts for very long... and perhaps the sorrow I felt in that moment of recognition of the truth was the last emotion I would ever truly know.

His answer was that there are no answers which do not create still more questions, and our search might well be an endless one ending only in futility.

But I looked out the window, following his gaze as he watched an alien rocket settle slowly into its berth and belch out its last breath of flame before becoming nothing more than a pseudo-sunrise on a strange and jagged horizon.

I wondered if there were any gypsies on board.

My Crystal:

I have just finished reading this – the last of Fogg's novel, written on the night before we left Lazali. We are now bound for the Galactic Fringe and the worlds Man has not yet reached. We will sleep for eleven years, and if we are fortunate, perhaps we shall not awaken at all. And... just maybe... I will be waiting for you on that alternate Earth you spoke of not so very long ago.

At any rate, if there are answers out there on the Fringe, or if there are gypsies, Fogg says that this has not all been in vain. I will write you of the children out there, and of their customs, and of their dreams, and their quests, which are probably not too different from those of any child on any world in any universe. It will not matter that you are no longer alive, my friend. Just as it does not matter that I am no longer alive myself. There are some things far worse than Death, and I believe you and I and Fogg have found some of them.

I know this will not be an easy thing for you to accept, nor do I expect you will write me again once you have read what is contained within this transmission. I had thought I was something more than human, and have discovered that I am, in fact, something less. I cannot return to Terra, for I am no longer the man you once knew; and though I understand that you would continue to love me always, I cannot give you less than I have given you in the past. I cannot give you memories without substance; I cannot say words with no meaning.

And if the ending is too sad, then I plead with you to reread those parts of Fogg's work which were about us, about our love, our happiness and our time together. Know that the man in those pages is the man who has loved you, and who will hopefully find an answer whereby he may experience life and love again.

And, finally, the man I have now become should remain forever as a stranger, for I fear you would not find much of value in him. Perhaps this is what the gods intended when they moved heaven in the middle of some black, black night – that we should be forever in search of it and never find it and never be able to keep that which is most important to all living beings.

I wish you warmth and love, and a life-long experience of both, my friend – an experience that will withstand the tests of magic and Man. Put them in a green bottle and place it on the hearth above the fire... and know that I will think of you always.

Until...
Raine
Communication #825HDCTerminate.END

About the Author...

Della Van Hise is a native of Florida, transplanted to California at the age of 21, who has subsequently sunk her roots into the high desert near Joshua Tree National Park. She has not personally seen any aliens since around 1992, but there is rumored to be a secret UFO base underneath her house.

Her first professional novel was best-selling KILLING TIME – the controversial Star Trek novel which was recalled and re-edited in 1984. More recently, Della has written extensively in the non-fiction genre, with titles such as QUANTUM SHAMAN: DIARY OF A NAGUAL WOMAN and SCRAWLS ON THE WALLS OF THE SOUL. If you enjoyed the works of Carlos Castaneda or Don Miguel Ruiz, you'll enjoy the non-fiction works of Della Van Hise.

In addition, Della has written professionally for Tomorrow Magazine and other prominent science fiction publications. Her most recent fiction works include Sons of Neverland (an award-winning literary novel); Year of the Ram (a space-faring gay romance); and Coyote (a – romantic science fiction novel combining the mystical aspects of martial arts, coming of age, and personal sacrifice.)

Other fiction titles from Eye Scry Publications...

NO FORWARDING ADDRESS
Della Van Hise

When Terrans came to sail dark seas,
And see what stars might be...
Heaven moved with no forwarding address,
And left this void to me.
(Children's song from Lazali)

———————

A literary science fiction novel told in the voice of an empath, *No Forwarding Address* explores the lures and the dangers of love, the tragedies and triumphs stirring in the human heart.

When Crystal and Raine first meet, it is 50 years after The Great War on Earth. They are hesitant to trust, afraid to love. But even if they are able to overcome these seemingly insurmountable obstacles, is even love enough?

When a man has the stars in his eyes, legend says he must serve them above all others.

———————

I knew then that it wasn't love and hate who were mirror twins. The final irony was that <u>grief</u> would always turn out to be the paradoxical antithesis and simultaneous manifestation of whatever it is what humans call love.

Crystal remained silent and walked a few steps away from Raine – further down the shoreline, until she stood under the wing of one fallen Phantom. She thought of the ship she had seen from the balcony of our home, and though it had long since disappeared over the dark and treacherous abyss of the ocean, its image lingered clearly in her thoughts. On that ship was a man, she thought. A terribly lonely man who made no great difference to the flow of time or the memory of the galaxy. A man who, like Raine, was compelled to keep moving and look only ahead and never behind. A man who could not afford the luxury of waving goodbye to friends on shore.

At last, she turned toward her beloved and watched him watching the darkness. He stood only a few feet away, yet the images in my mind said he might as well have been a million light years off in the void. He was lost to her in that instant out-of-time, just as lost and impossible to find as the light from that ship which had vanished over the horizon...

www.eyescrypublications.com
http://www.amazon.com/Forwarding-Address-Della-Van-Hise-ebook/dp/B00PEOSKJ0/

COYOTE
Della Van Hise

A Novel of Love, Honor
and Personal Sacrifice...

When River Willows is accused of a murder she didn't commit, her life takes a turn toward the sanctuary of a world existing at right-angles to our own. Combining the mysticism of martial arts and the romantic conflict of a young woman torn between two powerful men, COYOTE takes the reader on an epic journey of dangerous secrets, military cover-ups, and the infinite heart of the peaceful warrior.

――――――――――――

"So who's Coyote?" I asked, trying to ignore the effect he was having on me. "You?"

Steale laughed easily, though it did little to hide the torment behind that mask of indifference he wore so well.

"Coyote's a scavenger, Jack of all trades. The Native Americans call him the trickster - the one who brought chaos down on the world." He shrugged as if altogether unconcerned. "Original sin."

"Is that what you are?" I asked, keeping it light despite the growing knot my stomach. "Original sin?"

He kept his profile to me, eyes straight ahead as he drove. "Sure you want to know?"

I couldn't help wondering if I had cornered the coyote, or if the clever trickster had cornered me.

――――――――――――

By the author of **KILLING TIME** – without a doubt the most controversial **STAR TREK** novel ever published!

From the author:
www.eyescrypublications.com

On Amazon
http://www.amazon.com/Coyote-Della-Van-Hise/dp/0976689782/

YEAR OF THE RAM
Della Van Hise

Year of the Ram was described by one reviewer as... "A spacefaring gay romance full of love, angst, and longing."

Only after Star Commander Morgan Diego becomes an exile as a result of a Galaxy Corps political blunder does he begin to realize how much he valued the companionship of his second in command - the mysterious Lucien, an Alfarian who is more elven than human, with peculiar powers & abilities which begin to unfold as he, too, realizes what he has lost.

Separated by circumstance from his former life, Morgan is thrust into a world where he must survive by his wits. When he meets a peculiar little old man calling himself Kim Le, Morgan finds himself in a situation where he is required to master The Art - not only a form of human & extraterrestrial martial arts, but a way of living and being that will alter his life forever.

At the temple, he is introduced to his new teacher, another Alfarian who begins to steal his heart - a heart which is already promised to Lucien. Torn and conflicted, Morgan struggles with the world he left behind and the world he now inhabits.

Beginning to believe he may never again return to his ship and to the friends and loved ones he left behind, he is all the more frustrated and heartbroken when a new Master arrives at the temple: a man to whom Morgan is immediately drawn both mentally and physically, a man who is strikingly familiar... yet utterly alien.

Year of the Ram is a fully-fleshed novel, approximately 97000 words, with a focus on the love story and romance angle. Set against a science fiction milieu, it explores the infinite possibilities of the human and alien heart. Sexual content is explicit, though is not the primary focus of the novel.

For those who like a romance that forces its characters to contemplate the ecstasies AND the agonies of love... you will enjoy *Year of the Ram* immensely.

FROM THE AUTHOR:
www.eyescrypublications.com
ON AMAZON:
http://www.amazon.com/Year-Ram-Della-Van-Hise/dp/0989693813/

LETTERS TO AN ANDROID
Wendy Rathbone

Cobalt is a created human, vat grown and born adult, with no human rights and indentured to serve others for the duration of his life. Liyan is a young man with wanderlust in his eyes, embarking on a career that takes him to the furthest regions of space. The two become unlikely friends and create a memorable long-distance correspondence. Through Liyan, Cobalt gets to explore the universe, living vicariously through his friend's wave transmissions. A strong bond develops between them that not even the stars can put asunder.

Now you know an android who writes poetry.

This is all your fault. Did you not read my last wave telling you extracurricular activities for my kind are discouraged? Of course this is harmless and strangely enjoyable and does not necessarily require me to leave the hotel. Pel would not care if I wrote lines of equations or nonsensical juxtaposed words. As long as the act does not bring my mental state into question.

However, in history, poetry is often written by the rebels.

So we can keep this to ourselves.

Let me know about your lieutenant's test.

And to give you peace of mind, I never believed you observed me as anything other than human.

Some people are and always will be hateful bigots. Most people are simply uncomfortable in speaking to "property." And anyway, friendship, like poetry, is also discouraged.

Your friend,
Cobalt

FROM THE AUTHOR:
www.eyescrypublications.com

ON AMAZON:
http://www.amazon.com/Letters-Android-Wendy-Rathbone/dp/0989693872/

PALE ZENITH
Wendy Rathbone
A Science Fiction Novel

On a far-flung "Earth" in a parallel universe, two factions are fighting a decades-long psychic war. Young talented psychics are being temporarily kidnapped from present day Earth, seemingly at random, to serve as part of one side's psychic army. They are put under the control of spychiatrists, mysterious machines with many limbs that have a programmed ability to travel time and space and universes to kidnap and control carefully selected humans. The humans never know they are being used; when their missions are completed they are brought back to their universe through time and placed back in their beds, their memories wiped.

_____

The shadows wound the tall corridor in muted gold, varnished brown. It seemed as though they were in the bowels of a giant serpent coiled outside time, outside space.

When they left the palace, a familiar sun flourished in a clear, blue sky. But this wasn't their sun. Not Zack's sun. It was an alien star burning within a different galaxy in an all too distant universe. Zack looked up squinting, trying to see if he could peer beyond the sky, beyond the pale of midday and into his own timespace, but there was nothing. Only sunlight. Only the thin atmosphere of an Earth not his own.

His back knotted again. Leo's presence was a gelid space inside his chest, empty. Always before he'd felt a warmth there, a sort of pressure like someone's hand pressed gently to his heart. He'd taken Leo for granted knowing, the way a shadow falls when you block the sun, that he was there around him, inside him: blood, air, salt, brain, soul. They were genetic duplicates, twins, spiritual halves. Without him, Zack knew the first icy tugs of panic.

FROM THE AUTHOR
www.eyescrypublications.com
ON AMAZON
http://www.amazon.com/Pale-Zenith-Wendy-
Rathbone/dp/0976689790/

The Foundling
by Wendy Rathbone

Diego is a powerful man with a tragic past. Out on the expansive ocean in his private yacht, he discovers a beautiful and mysterious man adrift on a raft, near death. The bond that forms between them in the aftermath of Alec's rescue is one of fierce passion, though lacking in trust. Can they make it work, or will Alec's amnesia bring forth secrets so disturbing as to tear them apart? A passionately erotic love story of desire and darkness, exquisite and explicit.

_____

I can see his struggle between gratitude and uneasiness. He is buffeted by all things new and strange. He does not know where he is from, who he is or what happened to him. He does not know me. There has not been enough time to transition between strangers and friendship.

This isolation of his is something I can identify with, but it is also a feeling no one can help him with until or unless he gets his own life back. And his memory.

If that doesn't happen, then it will take time for him to build a new life. He is polite to me, even friendly, but even a night together during a storm with his arms wrapped tight around my waist doesn't calm the surge I see inside him, the emptiness, the loss, possibly even panic. That night may have reinforced some trust in me, but so far not enough for him to completely relax.

He seeks me out, though. That's something. He sits by me at dinner when he can have any seat of his choosing. I watch him closely when he does not realize it. At dinner the following night after we had only 'slept' together, and before we go to bed again in separate rooms, I notice everything about him, how he moves, the way the air warms when he is closer to me, the dry sheen of his lips as they part for more air when he is reacting to something, or speaking, or eating.

His hands still shake. Anyone else might not notice because he keeps them clasped into fists at his sides or, while sitting, pressed tight to his lap.

I spend another fretful night alone. I dream restlessly, wild, loud and colorful visions I cannot recall at all as soon as my eyes open. All I know is the dreams leave me unfulfilled, impatient.

www.eyescrypublications.com

None Can Hold the Dark
Wendy Rathbone

In the eagerly-awaited sequel to Wendy Rathbone's homoerotic romance ***The Foundling,*** Diego and Alec meet new challenges in private and from the outside world. Diego is being investigated by the local police for murder. Meanwhile, Alec's amnesia and the trauma of his kidnapping by white slavers continue to plague him. And the danger to Alec is not yet over.

Distracted by their new love, both men fail to see certain threats until it is almost too late.

———————————

"Why do you keep doing this illegal business?" Now Alec's gaze turned toward him, open as the day and lit with a sad frenzy, a challenge. "You could go anywhere, do anything, be anyone."

Diego had asked himself that question on rare occasions. In truth, he got used to what he was, what he did. Even a dangerous known was perhaps preferable to the unknown. "People depend on me."

Alec shook his head, but smiled a little as he said, "That's so weak." He leaned forward, over the arm of the chair, and put his shaking hand on the back of Diego's head. The kiss was cool, lingering, moist with salt. When Alec pulled back, he said almost matter of factly, "It's like there's sharks and there's goldfish and one can't decide to become the other."

Diego was still stunned by the kiss. But the words hit him hard. In them was the unfair conjecture of a locked fate. He believed in making his own fate...or luck. Did Alec think only one kind of man lived inside him and that was all there was to it? To life? It hurt. Badly.

Diego sat back on his heels, catching himself with his hands on the smooth floor. "So, Alec, which am I?"

Alec frowned.

Diego said, "I made choices in my life. I made them No one made them for me. If I need to be strong I'm strong. If I need to be vicious I can be that too. So what? I'm stuck there? In a pattern, a role...with no free will?"

Alec watched him inquisitively now.

"Because," Diego went on, "I'm solely responsible for my actions. Me. Could you say the same of the shark?"

They both waited, the silence covering them in muggy discomfort.

"You think you understand me?" Diego finally asked.

www.eyescrypublications.com

My House Is Full of Whispers
Wendy Rathbone

Ten erotica short stories by Wendy Rathbone - former winner of the prestigious WRITERS OF THE FUTURE contest!

Leda has not one beautiful man, but two. Kale enters a secret world in a wealthy man's basement. Noah is in love with a man who hates sex. Dina lives next door to a famous Hollywood director she secretly loves. Dorian has a sixteen year old female student coming onto him. Tara is haunted by an erotic ghost. Young Dimitri is kidnapped by lecherous men. And more.

Author's Preface

When I wrote these stories, I deliberately set out to gently break down certain barriers, and I've certainly broken taboos. Do I care? No. This is fantasy at its purest level. The stories are never meant to be political statements, nor do they make any attempt at political correctness, and there is little consideration for safe sex. While I definitely condone safe sex, my stories come from fictional realities in my head where safe sex is not much of a concern because, well, it's imaginary and it's fiction!

For me, these stories are meant as little poetic erotic ramblings merely to stir the flames of desire, nothing more. They are pure fantasy and therefore to be enjoyed as such. Every story is erotic in nature, meant to titillate, some more explicit than others. Some of the stories are light, some are darker. I invite the reader to a feast of diversity and delight.

One reader commented: "...some of the most beautifully written erotica since Anais Nin!"

FROM THE AUTHOR: www.eyescrypublications.com
ON AMAZON:
http://www.amazon.com/House-Full-Whispers-Wendy-Rathbone-ebook/dp/B00IJK3G04/

UNEARTHLY
by Wendy Rathbone

A Collection of
Award-Winning Poetry

Intro by the Author: This book contains all my out of print chapbooks (mini-collections of an author's work usually published by smaller presses.)

The chapbooks published within include: **Moon Canoes**, published by Dark Regions Press, 1994

(Im)mortal, published by Shadowfire Press, 1996
Scrying The River Styx, published by Anamnesis Press, 1999
Autumn Phantoms, published by Flesh and Blood Press, 2000
Dreams of Decadence Presents: Wendy Rathbone, published by DNA Publications 2002
Dancing in the Haunted Woodlands, published by Yellow Bat Review, 2003
Vampyria, published by Eye Scry Publications, 2005

She Sleeps With Vampires
She sleeps with vampires
courting velvet breaths
poem-dreams
chill-stopped hearts

Wrapped in her arms
like teddy bear thoughts
purple lips trembling
at her quiet throat
they love her more than
somber rain
more than autumn
more than ash-soft hearths of night.

FROM THE AUTHOR
www.eyescrypublications.com

ON AMAZON
http://www.amazon.com/Unearthly-Wendy-Rathbone-ebook/dp/B00B0MTIZK/

Non-fiction titles from Eye Scry Publications...

TEACHINGS OF THE IMMORTALS
by Mikal Nyght

So... You Want To Live Forever?
The teachings are presented as brief vignettes in no particular order of importance. This is not a book you read from start to finish in a single night. It is a grimoire of self-creation, intended to be contemplated slowly so as to be assimilated wholly. Pick it up and turn to a page at random. Where your eyes come to rest on the page is your lesson for the day. Go no further until you have assimilated the lesson totally.

The teachings are seduction as much as instruction. This is the way of The Dark Evolution.

Two Brief Excerpts...

The Ruby Slippers
The danger of the consensual continuum is that its natural gravity exists at the lowest common denominator of human experience, and because of this it will automatically make you forget those elusive truths you've fought to learn, and before you know it you're lost in petty dramas again, sinking into the mire of old familiar scripts.

The only way to overcome this is to be continually cavorting with worlds and events beyond human experience, journeying into the unknown so that it can become known, expanding knowledge and awareness to become more than you were, bringing back from the Dreaming those secrets which will teach you how to use the ruby slippers to transport yourself over the rainbow to the vampyre wizard's secret lair.

Perception
This is the nature of reality: to be precisely what perception dictates, as solid and whole as your interpretation of it, or as changeable and eternal as you permit it to be.

It wasn't knowledge god tried to keep from Man, you see. It was perception, for perception alone has the power to destroy god and obliterate comfortable consensual realities to create unending immortality.

Take the apple, my embryonic children. Nibble its red red flesh. Open your vampyre eyes so you may finally begin to *See*.

FROM THE AUTHOR http://www.immortalis-animus.com

Quantum Shaman:
Diary of a Nagual Woman
Della Van Hise

"Diary of a Nagual Woman brings a quantum understanding to what has traditionally been believed to be a mystical path alone. This book picks up where Carlos Castaneda left off to take us on a roller coaster ride of our own forgotten power..."
- Michael Grove, Independent Reviewer

_____

When I asked how Orlando had known I would come to this remote location, and how he himself had gotten there – since there were no other cars in the tiny parking lot – he only smiled a little, stretched out his long legs, and slouched down on that cold metal bench to stare up at the stars.

"You're predictable," he said as if I should have already known. "I'm here because this is where you always come when you're mad at the world."

I attempted to engage him in a conversation of just exactly how he knew I was mad at the world, since I'd had no direct contact with him in quite some time, nothing to give him any hint of what was going on in my everyday life. But even as I began spelling all of that out to him, he brushed my words aside.

"Do you want to talk or do you want to waste time looking for logical explanations for every magical thing that ever happens?" he asked. "That's what's wrong with the world, you know. Instead of embracing the mysteries and trying to determine how they might open a crack in an otherwise humdrum, pre-programmed existence, people waste their entire lives explaining it all away, attaching labels to it, filing and categorizing it until it loses any meaning."

He had a point. And I'd already been inundated with enough mysteries in my time to know that some things simply had no explanation humans could understand. *'Magic is only science not yet understood'*. Words Orlando had written more than a year before rattled through my mind up there in the middle of the night, in the middle of nowhere, looking down on a world that seemed far more unreal to me at that moment than the world he had been trying to teach me to *see*.

He was there – whether physically or in some spirit-form manifestation is ultimately of no importance, for in the sorcerer's world there is no difference between body and spirit, and in any world, perception is reality.

FROM THE AUTHOR
www.quantumshaman.com

Scrawls On the Walls
of the Soul

By the author of
QUANTUM SHAMAN

Scrawls on the Walls of the Soul
Della Van Hise

The long-awaited follow-up to
Quantum Shaman: Diary of a Nagual Woman.
Stands alone, or order together!

"If you've ever felt like a stranger in a strange land, this book is your road map to survival in the spiritual wilderness!" (Michael Grove)

~

It was May of 2000 when my mentor threw me out of the quantum cosmic classroom and said, "I've taught you everything I can. Now it's time to take that knowledge and slam it up against the walls of the real world. If it remains intact and survives the brutality to which it will be subjected, you will get a gold star next to your name and be allowed to proceed to the next level." No mention was made of what this next level might be, or if, indeed, it truly existed.

Go ahead – try to explain this all-consuming path to your friends and relatives. They will smile politely, squirm uncomfortably, and eventually they will stop returning your phone calls and look the other way when they see you coming. And who can blame them? They live in the real world with their office jobs and nuclear families and a host of mindless sitcoms waiting on the propaganda box at the end of their busy day. In direct contrast, it could be observed that anyone who has dedicated themselves to the pursuit of forbidden knowledge really doesn't live in that world at all. Not for lack of wanting, perhaps, but because the real world is quickly seen to be little more than a series of programs and illusions – not unlike The Matrix. And not surprisingly, the people who populate that world may begin to take on a peculiar zombie-like quality.

You find yourself alone in a world of jesters, jokers and jackasses. Now what?

FROM THE AUTHOR
www.quantumshaman.com

ON AMAZON
http://www.amazon.com/Scrawls-Walls-Soul-Della-Hise-ebook/dp/B008CUKH6C/

Eye Scry Publications
A Visionary Publishing Company
www.eyescrypublications.com